PROMISE UNTO DEATH

By Grace Cash

HERALD PRESS / SCOTTDALE, PENNSYLVANIA

PROMISE UNTO DEATH

This book is lovingly dedicated

To the memory of my cousin—

Rebecca Cash (1950-1966)

Some ambassadors are prematurely recalled from their posts, after a brief but shining service, and so was Rebecca Cash at the age of sixteen years. She lived among us as though God walked with her, and the impact of her Christian influence will be felt from generation to generation.

> "Take from me all earthly ties,
>   All my goods reclaim;
> But let me die, and leave to earth
>   A good and righteous name." °

°The above poem by Grace Cash, published in 1956 in *The Young People's Journal*, Nazarene Publishing House, Kansas City, Missouri, reprinted in this memorial by special permission.

1

☐ THE SMALL VALLEY TOWN lay cradled inside the scalloped sidings of vast mountains. Its church spires rose like purifiers into the blue and white chiffon clouds of the August morning. This was Loganville, with its narrow valley roads and its graduated green hills.

Kent Wilson watched his wife's face, marking her first reaction to his native town, and a frown deepened the slight lines etching his forehead. Maybe she would get used to it—this parochial pocket in the hills. But he watched her face grow pensive as she looked out her side window of the new sleek station wagon.

It was not an ordinary face, he was well aware of that, but he had never intended to choose an ordinary wife. After a month's honeymoon on the

5

coast, he still marveled at her spontaneous gaiety, her vivacious good humor. Prior to that she had been Miss Jo Adcox, secretary, like a hundred other women who had accompanied their employers to the annual merchants' convention.

"Welcome to Loganville, my pretty Jo," Kent said now, as they approached the business section. "It may not look like much, but you'll get used to it. It's an old town, what there is of it. My grandfather built my house—our house—over a hundred years ago."

She laughed and his heart quickened at the sound of her bell-toned laughter. "I'm afraid I married above myself," she said. "Dad could barely afford rent on a walk-up flat. But then it didn't matter. Most of the time he was on a merchant ship. They should never have married. Mother disliked being pinned down. I can't remember much of it except with sadness. We separated, each going a different way. And then Mother and Dad died the same year my brothers and I left home." She talked frequently of her past but each time with variations.

He slowed the car and pulled her briefly toward him. "I'm sorry, Jo," he said. "My mother believed a Christian was better off with God when the time came to leave this world."

"You know, Kent, my parents didn't believe such nonsense. And you know I don't."

"They taught you, as you are," he said, apologizing for her, excusing her, and yet careful to conceal that he believed she stood in need of apology. That was the unstated part of the promise which

6

if kept, might insure a happy marriage. But if the promise were broken—Kent thought no further of such impossibles.

"Not exactly," she corrected. "They were seeking something all their lives. Sometimes they went to church and took us. But they couldn't get the drift of religion. I knew all the time there was no reality in faith and prayer and all those ceremonies. Maybe if they'd been really smart, they'd not have shopped around in the first place."

His mouth closed tightly. Maybe he should say something, but he disliked any argument with this prize he had won—this most beautiful of women.

"Then you do regret my life?" she asked. "You really wanted a Christian wife?"

"I wanted you as you are," he answered quickly. How could he explain? If she would not come to him except he made a promise unbreakable this side the grave, then he must consistently keep the promise. Besides, he needed her, to survive the perpetual torture of his mind. He was an indirect murderer and his sin lay in his bosom, unforgiven, heavy, burdensome.

When the trains rumbled through the smoky valley town, sounding their dreary short-long-short blasts, he remembered Cecil.

He remembered Cecil driving the Shedd's first car, bought at a used car lot, the final installment paid the week before. Invariably he remembered Cecil driving into the siding of a freight train. He had never been able to forgive himself for his part in the tragedy. Nor could he ever forget that terrible eternity-in-a-moment tragic accident.

A college student at the time, Kent indulged in frequent motor races on the public highways and it was he who initiated drag racing in Loganville. Afterward there were more wild oats to sow, there was the devil in him to show off, bidding for the admiration of women and the scornful head-shaking of gray-haired old men. Yet people died unexpectedly every day. The thought mitigated his conscience, and yet there was no blotting out the traumatic results of his selfish youth.

In high school he had been a leader, a bit arrogant and with more than a little pride. In college his concept of his worth had increased. Into none of this had God fitted. Excluding Him in everything, he had almost succeeded in his willful defection. Perhaps he could have done so entirely had it not been for Cole and Sadie Wilson.

"We're not on the map yet but we're aiming high," Kent said, breaking the silence. He kept his eyes intently on the road as it twisted and angled, splitting the smoky railroad town into halves. He pointed out various places of merchandise, including those with the Wilson imprint. "It's still a bit primitive and small-town, but I think you'll find just about everything you'll need here. Even a hotel." He pointed out the Town Inn, a rather shabby two-story boarding house for transients, or local loafers.

"I'm not apt to put up there," she said, shrugging her shoulders. She nodded toward the narrow hole-in-the-wall poolroom, PAW'S PLACE, a half block from the inn. "What about this spot, Kent?"

8

"The pool hall?" He glanced at the dark-windowed, narrow hall, filled the clock around with men, gambling greedily, compulsively, wildly. Operated by Paw Milligan, it was hated by many of Loganville's citizens. "I've been in only once and it's a rough place, my Jo."

"You may not go there, as you say, but what do you do for entertainment?"

"I'll see you're entertained fully," he promised evasively. "Money is no question; so you can have anything you wish for yourself."

Jo didn't answer and she was careful to check the slight regret she felt. An efficient secretary, she had earned sufficient money to provide all the things she wanted. From marriage there must be much more than money and things—much more.

"You can open a charge account at all the Winterville shops; so going to the trading post on Saturdays will be easier for you," he said. "Of course, everybody goes to the county seat on Saturday."

"That should be fun," she said still considering what she hoped to achieve from this marriage. In a moment of nostalgia for the familiar, she was stricken with the spiraling fate that had brought her to this dreary town. Mushrooming up from an odd assortment of houses and businesses, lofty church steeples lent the town a hint of majesty. Aloud she said, "I've counted three churches, so far."

"That's all we have, except the summer tents," Kent replied, wondering why he had failed to notice until now that her eyes were the green of early spring onions. The thought amused him and he stored

9

it away as an anecdote for a future party they planned to give at their house. "In April the Holy unto God people held a tent meeting over there."

"Then the worshipers are holy?"

"For all I know," he answered. "They call it 'revival' meeting. The public is invited. See that hill, past Little Points railroad crossing? See that space surrounded by a circlet of pines? That's where another group is putting up right now. They come in August every year."

"When will it begin?"

"This coming Sunday. Sometimes they stay till snow has frosted Old Brass Bald," he answered, pointing to the green-foliaged mountain they had come by. "It's the same every summer except that the leaders change. This year it's Reverend Neal Redmond from Marble Hill, South Carolina. He's a radio minister, very outspoken. I've tuned in on his program. Some of our own townspeople attend the tent revivals but mostly the crowds come from the countryside. They come from everywhere."

Jo suspected that the congregation would be composed mainly of her sort of people, very middle-class people. The Adcoxes, whether coastal or inland, whether religious or heathen, inhabited the earth. Then she quipped, "People with no place to go."

"These people claim they're going straight to heaven." He grinned and winked at her. "But then some of Loganville's most pious charter members think they have reservations, too."

"I'll go to church with you," she stated impulsively. "Whatever else I do, I shall be seen in church."

That thought had just occurred to her. She knew the habit would be good socially. She did want to endear herself to Kent's friends. "What are the people like, Kent?"

He waved to a heavyset man in brown khaki and a bill cap, leaning against the Greymount Bus Station. "Well, let's begin with Old Tobe," he said. "He's the mayor, sheriff, chief counselor, and baby-sitter for the town. Look at him. That's what he's like."

Jo tilted her head and laughed heartily, revealing a set of teeth perfect in form but inset haphazardly. Then quickly, turning serious, she asked, "No, what are they really like?"

A frown traced his lean handsome profile and he felt in every nerve of his body the sudden reminder that the time would come when she would discover the dark secrets of his own life. In spite of current customs that winked at a double standard, in the quiet intimate moments when a man had taken a wife, how could he keep back the shadows of his past life? He moved his long legs to quiet his nervous impulses which he suffered occasionally. The people did not concern him, so long as they kept out of his affairs. Some openly resented him; some envied him. Some ignored him. But he had to answer her question.

"The people are like people anywhere in the world, I guess. Good, bad, gay, mad. Except for one thing. I expect no area in the world, since Nazareth, has had more religious fanatics than Kensington County. No doubt, they'll witness to you about your personal salvation. They do the same for all unchurched people; so I want you to understand, honey."

She sighed. Reared in a family of brothers, the only daughter, she had never known anything other than enthusiastic acceptance, just as she was, the gay one, the life of the party. The first twenty years of her life she had been accepted with these qualities, but Loganville impressed her as something entirely foreign to the coast. "I'll try to conform— a little," she said, repulsed at the thought, but to please him she promised. Marriage seemed to be a continuous chain of compromises.

Kent brightened, considering that Jo, the small bundle of beauteous energy, would diminish his gloom. The people, coolly aloof to him since Cecil's tragic death, would be charmed with Jo, whom they would never completely understand—but neither, for that matter, did he.

"They'll think you're the prettiest bride ever to set foot in Loganville," he said. "They'll copy you, the way you walk, talk, dress, and act. Even what you cook and eat. They'll think you're the greatest; they can't help themselves."

Suddenly her attention switched to a garden of perennials, planted thick in front of a shabby yellow house on Grape Avenue. "Look, dear! Aren't they pretty?"

"Yes," he answered. "Mrs. Duncan planted them."

"Who is she?"

"Mrs. Minnie Duncan. A widow before I was born. She died the first of June this year."

"How old was she?"

"Eighty. She was a charter member of the First

12

Church and a lifetime Sunday school teacher." He grinned. "I guess the best of us are a little calculating. She left a stipulation about the flowers. She knew she would die before the flowers did; so she asked that everybody who stopped to admire the garden kneel a moment to pray for a lost soul."

"Oh," Jo said with a slight grimace. She need not stop in the garden. She was probably a lost soul herself—if there was such a thing.

At the central railroad crossing Kent stopped for a red signal. Fourteen people had died as a result of the trains passing directly through the town and the people had come to dread the dreary spasmodic whistles, as the trains slithered around the curves, halting at each intersection only slightly, to signal for right of way. Neither passengers nor cargo were accommodated at Loganville and serving the town no purpose, the railroad was considered a nuisance.

Kent and Jo sat quietly until the freight train clattered past, the wheels sharply clack-clacking, the flagmen waving white-gloved hands.

When the noise subsided, Jo shifted uneasily in her seat. "Everything's gray. This is a sad town, Kent. But maybe towns inhabited by Christians are supposed to be sad."

"Come now, wait till you know the town's possibilities," he said. "It's waiting for you to show the people how to live it up."

"I'll try," she promised. She wanted happiness, not only for herself but for those around her. She had no conception of happiness in solitude. If she were to be happy and gay here, then others would

13

have to do as she did, she knew. "Doing something irregular keeps me healthy. It keeps me from thinking and remembering."

"Don't think," Kent said, scowling as a double-deck Greymount bus swerved past him heading toward the Greymount Bus Station.

"Let's drop by Sally Baxley's house," he suggested, when they reached a road fork. "She's someone you should meet and she'll scalp me if I don't bring you by."

"All right," she agreed.

"Soon you'll meet Miss Lizbeth Lambert." He did not tell her that Lizbeth had not spoken to him since her fiancé, Cecil Shedd, had been killed in an automobile race with him. It had never bothered him a great deal but now it seemed regrettable. "She manages Greymount Station but she spends most of her time in church work."

She shook her head and laughed, her dark lustrous hair fanning about her face. "You wear so many masks, Kent. I can't figure you out."

2

□ A MOUNTAIN TRAILS BUS, the motor revving, made ready for its journey north as the driver backed into the parking lot at the Greymount Bus Station. Over the noise of engines and horns sounded the clear-toned voice of Lizbeth Lambert, magnified by the loudspeaker: "Bus to Johnston, Winterville, Gladstone, and points north departing. Last call. Last call, all points north, destination New York. Departure time nine-fifteen. All passengers aboard. Last call."

Passengers dispersed noisily with their baggage. After a short interval Lizbeth announced the arriving bus and the fifteen-minute rest stop. She jotted a row of figures on the schedule ledger, then hurried toward the serving counter. Pouring ice water into a dozen glasses waiting on a tray, she took orders from travelers and relayed them by waitress-code, to Mrs. Ina Powers, her assistant and chief cook. She then moved down the aisles by the faded green wallside booths, serving anxious transients.

"Well, I see Greymount's still thriving," a gray-uniformed bus driver remarked, settling lazily into the last vacant seat. He surveyed Lizbeth, admiring her clean mountain finesse but marveling that anyone confined to a few square miles of territory could apparently be contented.

He had married a tall slender girl who looked strikingly like Lizbeth. Except that Brenda was a chic brunette and wore sophisticated clothes, not the cotton printed skirts and white blouses which somehow seemed right for this honey-blond girl, at twenty-four still utterly refreshing. Winking a well-trained black eye at her, he added, "No wonder Greymount thrives. Look at the princess running it."

Lizbeth smiled gratefully. She had heard every remark imaginable, both honorable and insinuating, during the six years she had managed Greymount. After graduating from Loganville High School, she buried her dreams for a bachelor of science degree in teaching and started work at the bus station. Considering her invalid mother's needs, she could hardly have found anything more fitting than the station's split shifts. Widowed in Lizbeth's senior high school year, Mrs. Lambert depended on her for all that Ashton Lambert had once done so devotedly.

"What's cookin', sweet?" the driver asked.

She turned off the small brown radio and handed him the sandwich menu. He knew what sandwiches were available but he glanced politely at the limited and unvarying assortment. Made at the counter by Lizbeth or her assistant, the salads, soups, pies, beverages, steaming coffee had all been prepared with the utmost care. An industrious manager, Lizbeth provided adequate sustenance for travelers in transit through the mountains, going south to the agricultural and industrial centers, or north to points as remote as Nova Scotia.

"Make it ham and lettuce on rye. And a big slice of lemon meringue pie and a coke."

"Thank you, Mr. Franklin." She made a quick note on her pad. "I'm glad you're back on your job. And I know you're glad to be out of the hospital."

He groaned. "I had it. A whole month flat on my back. They thought a while I wouldn't make it."

She started on, needing to rush, but turned back to say quietly, "I did remember you. I remembered you in prayer."

He sat forward. "Thanks, Miss Lambert. I'm surprised you remembered me."

"I couldn't forget you needed prayer at a time like that," she answered. "At any time we all need God."

"We sure do," he agreed. "Thanks again."

She went to the counter, her heart beating rapidly because she had witnessed to another driver, a difficult feat, these men being wise in the ways of the world. Physically he reminded her of Kent Wilson but the resemblance ended there. Kent wore the

17

badge of wealth. Like his parents, like the parents before them, he had been nurtured on Christian principles, but these he had thrown to the four winds in his early youth. Lately he had developed an addiction for the feel of money. Only time would tell what direction he would follow now that he had married a strange woman, a coastal native.

"Two cokes over here," a young man called from a rear booth. "And two hot dogs."

On her pad Lizbeth noted "Two hot dogs cold," knowing that travelers avoided onions. She knew as much about transients as some women know about babies.

Dispatching the driver's order, she took another from an anxious mother traveling with three small children. Next she carried the double hot dog order to the back booth, where she recognized Stu Hambrick and Bob Connors, both current journalism students at Winterville State College.

"Hi," the young men said in unison, but Stu, glancing mischievously at her, added, "I imagine at a place like this a woman can meet lots of eligible men."

"Stu's imagination is the biggest thing about him," Bob remarked.

"Well, imagination's all right. Paul had a fine imagination," she said, as though the thought so recently occurring had surprised her. "God used him in a glorious way. I think He must have a special purpose for one with an active imagination."

"Like Stu, you mean?" Incredulous, Bob looked from Lizbeth to his companion. "I'm not being facetious but how could God possibly use him?"

"God could use anyone who wants to be used,"
she answered, and hurried to a waiting customer.
In this manner she witnessed daily to dozens of
people, some who were devout Christians and many
who neither knew nor cared for anything relating
to God.

At two o'clock Ina Powers whisked in, bursting
with news. Tying on a brief red-checked apron, she
asked, "Have you heard the latest? Kent Wilson
has arrived in town with his wife. They stopped at
Mrs. Baxley's. He wanted her to meet his wife and
you know her! She promptly asked her when she
expected to join Kent's church. I think she meant
when would she have her church letter transferred,
and you know what? This new Mrs. Wilson told
them she didn't believe a single thing ever written
about God."

"Ina, that can't be true. Don't believe everything
you hear," Lizbeth said, her voice a husky stunned
whisper. "Kent has a few Christian scruples left,
I'm sure."

"Oh, no, this is straight—shocking but straight. And
serves that conceited sheik right; just what he needed."

"You shouldn't feel like that," Lizbeth said. "It
isn't our place to seek vengeance."

"All right then. It's your grave he's walking over,
not mine." Ina smiled, showing tiny teeth. A frail,
petite woman, early married, early a mother of three
small children and prematurely widowed, she now
handled a man-sized job as household breadwinner.

"Never mind, Ina. You just think about how the

Lord wants you to consider Kent and his wife," Lizbeth advised gently.

What she said appeared as one thing; what she truly felt, another. If Ina knew—if they all knew—how she despised Kent Wilson and all that concerned him, her Christian witness would end abruptly.

Going to the door, Lizbeth gazed over the wasteland of Old Brass Bald, a massive catchall for the elements. Rain, frost, snow, sleet beat against its sides as it stood there, year after year, silent, sullen. For Lizbeth, Kent Wilson's return rolled back time and it was a May morning less than six years ago that Cecil Shedd died.

On the last Thursday of that May gray morning clouds rolled over the patch of pines beyond the Shedds' small weathered house. Lizbeth sat by the window unable to sleep, checking a late term paper. Her father had gone early to his truck-driving highway development job; her mother, not feeling well, was still asleep. Coming in from the north, the chill May winds fluttered the ruffled cottage curtains.

Our senior high year is almost gone, Lizbeth thought, with both elation and regret. Soon now Cecil and I will be high school graduates.

She had just finished her coffee when she saw Charley Shedd come swiftly toward the Lamberts' kitchen door. In his haste he left the car door swinging. She ran out, sensing something not right. The screen door slammed twice before it settled.

"What's wrong? What is it?" she cried, her voice jerking and trembling.

Charley stopped at the hedgerow and waited for

her, his face dead white and agitated, his dark eyes
ghastly with a sudden grief.

"Mr. Shedd, what is it?" she asked again. "What's
wrong?"

"Everything is wrong." His voice was harsh and
dry as he tried to prepare her for his message.
"I still don't believe it. Lizbeth, can you come? Right
away?"

"What—where?" She stopped uncertainly, seized
with dread.

"Cecil—the train hit his car," he said. "He wants
to see you before he dies. Come—to the hospital."

She did not wait for him to finish but turned to
lean against the old crab tree. Burying her face in
her hands, she sobbed bitterly—but briefly, knowing
Cecil's need for her. She went with Charley Shedd
to the Loganville Hospital and in that hour her
heart turned to stone, except for her love for God.
At least He had not been crowded out—not completely.

"Lizbeth, aren't you taking a break?" Ina broke
her reverie.

"Yes, oh, yes," she answered, grateful to be pulled
back to reality. Except for the relief hours in which
she slipped away to herself, she could not hold a
public job. She removed her crisp apron and hurried
from the station but not to go directly home. Instead,
she walked the broom sedge trail paralleling the railroad, out past the cemetery to Cecil's grave.

At the Wilson landline, south of Old Brass Bald,
stood a time-scabbed oak tree. On the tough trunk
Cecil had carved

CECIL LOVES LIZBETH

The train screamed suddenly—a routine warning that the long train had reached the bend, marked by a white cross where swift wheels had crushed the speeding Shedd automobile into a shabby mass of steel. Kent Wilson, also racing to the crossing, had managed to stop his car with only seconds to spare.

Since her fiance's fatal accident Lizbeth had hated both the railroad and the Ocmaha River, placid, shallow, but often overflowing its banks during the rainy winter months. Above all she had hated Kent and she had hated even more the necessity of keeping her smoldering hatred a secret. She wanted to shout to the mountaintops how she felt about Kent, who had indirectly raised a gate to all her dreams.

She stood a while at Cecil's grave, offering a brief prayer, ending it as usual, "And do help me in some way to keep my promise to Cecil. Help me to know how to bring his father to Thee. Amen."

Afterward she walked toward the Shedd house, taking the path by the old grain mill where she had played as a child. It would be her first visit in more than a month. She remembered when the Shedd family had first moved into the house on the hill across from the Tabernacle Church of the Redeemed. Unfailingly, Vi Shedd had taken her children, a daughter and two younger sons, to church each Sunday. But Charley boasted that he had not darkened a church door since he was married and would not unless carried there a dead body. Too many Christians, so-called, had proved unscrupulous and crooked.

At first Lizbeth had known little of this family,

but everything had changed when Cecil had carved the crude, arrow-pierced heart on an oak tree at their freshman school picnic the following spring. Three years later he had died, having lived long enough to ask her forgiveness and to exact a promise of her.

"Help Dad understand about God," he begged. "Tell him I'm sorry but everything is all right with me—now. It will be—for everybody—even you—if Dad can learn to know God."

She had promised and she had tried, but Charley Shedd remained a resolute agnostic. "Show me, prove it to me," he challenged Lizbeth whom he loved as a daughter. Six years had come and gone but things were far from right for him. Nor were they right for Lizbeth, alone and lonely. And things were certainly not right for Vi, whose mind had atrophied from relentless grief. Rational most of the daylight hours, at night she lost her equilibrium. When the midnight train whistled mournfully through Loganville, she screamed until Charley had soundproofed the bedroom where they slept in order not to disturb the neighbors.

Before this shattering tragedy, Vi had lost her daughter in childbirth and her only grandchild had been placed, by the irresponsible father, in a Toledo orphanage. The eldest son had died of a sniper's bullet in Korea. These things could never seem right to Lizbeth, nor could she imagine any circumstance that would make them fit right.

Nor was life easy for Mrs. Lambert, sitting in her wheelchair or lying propped on fat pillows. Crippled when she fell on an icy sidewalk ten years before, she now depended solely on Lizbeth for the necessities and small comforts that seemed to keep her content. Nothing seemed right for anyone unless it was her father who after a long illness with asthma, had died, his good-bye a smiling, "I see my Lord and Savior! I see Him!"

Now that the small white house, resting on a pine knoll, had come into view, she paused a moment, bowing her honey-colored head, and she prayed, "Father, the way is not clear. Help me find peace in Thy will. And help me in some way to forgive Kent. Amen."

Dry-eyed, she turned and hurried up the path from the river crossing. Topping the knoll, she turned left and walked with long strides out the broom sedge field.

3

☐ WHEN LIZBETH entered the yard, Vi stopped plucking fresh-washed clothes from the line. "We'll go in and have a cup of coffee," she said, one arm filled with soap-scented laundry, the other gathering her black cotton-checked apron into a clothespin holder.

Vi Shedd was a big woman, broad-shouldered, wide-hipped, and her legs in coarse cotton stockings had the same heavy lines as her ponderous body. Lizbeth never knew whether her chronic fatigue sprang from the weight of her body or from her agonized spirit. "All my bones ache; I'm so tired. But I'd like to talk a while."

"You've heard that Kent got married?" Lizbeth remarked, breaking a twig from the lilac tree, and holding it to her lips for a brief kiss. Lilacs would

25

forever be associated in her mind with love and death.

"Everybody's heard," Vi answered, as they went into the kitchen. "Charley's not told me much of what he hears with the men. Just to hear Kent's name, he gets stirred up. He hears it often enough now. People are talking."

A big honest man and an enemy to none more than himself, Charley had never liked Kent, but after Cecil's death he had literally hated him, dying a little each time he heard his name. Now his greatest consolation was Lizbeth, whom he guarded solicitously.

They stopped in the kitchen, a meager room with starched white curtains at the half windows. The floor had been scrubbed until tiny splinters showed in the corn wood. Vi set cups and saucers from the open-faced cupboard and poured coffee from a white galvanized pot. Looking at her, a stout woman of forty-four, none would guess that she slept tied to her husband and had done so since a year after Cecil's death.

In the course of a dozen years she had given up her three children to death but the house remained physically the same, even to the flower-printed dishes stacked in the cupboard. The sun, streaming through the small double-sashed windows, had the grayness of the bus drivers' uniforms, or so it seemed to Lizbeth now, watching Vi nervously pouring two cups of strong black coffee. Vi's voice slurred, dragging out the words, and there was no longer the birdlike quality to her speech. For Cecil's parents, and for

26

Lizbeth, too, life had lost its expectancy. Lizbeth was keenly aware of this and regretted it.

"Now you just sit there and tell me all about Kent's new wife," Vi said as she took a chair opposite Lizbeth at the table. The table and the cabinets—any number of items in this house—had been made by Charley's own hands. A carpenter by trade, as well as a carpenter at heart, he rested ill when his hands had no touch with wood. "Talk fast before Charley gets back," she whispered. "He despises Kent Wilson."

"It's possibly time we all stopped hating Kent," Lizbeth said gently. "However much at fault he may have been, I think it best we go on as though the Wilsons were nowhere around. Forget them."

"Forget Kent Wilson?" She laughed harshly. "Forget he killed my last living child! He's a demon. You mark my words, that little scatterbrained wife of his is a sight better than he is."

Lizbeth stirred sugar into her coffee, weighing Vi's words. An agnostic, unable to accept the inspired gospel as the full truth, Charley had never disparaged Cole and Sadie Wilson for what they believed. But he considered Kent a pretender, a hypocrite.

"I know how you and Mr. Shedd feel about Kent," Lizbeth said. "But that's over now. Everything is changing. I hardly know which way to turn."

"Better keep away from Kent and his wife," Vi advised.

Lizbeth sat silent. This was not the old Vi; this was the Vi whose mind had gone slowly, some word

27

out of place, a cry in the night, a gasp in a strategic gathering. This was not the same Vi who had planned proudly how she would become the best grandmother in Loganville. Vi had promised there would be no layette problems, no baby-sitting worries, for Lizbeth and Cecil if only they would give her plenty of grandchildren. She had wanted the sound of busy feet, shrill small voices, countless questions that not even a wise grandmother dared answer. This had been her obsession, blasted on a moonless, starless night.

The tragedy had increased Lizbeth's perception that God's ways are beyond human understanding. And she had held on—some can. Vi had lost a part of her sanity and Charley had vowed that if there was a God, He was a cruel God.

Aware that she had unconsciously waited a long time to answer, Lizbeth leaned over to clasp Vi's hand. "Don't worry," Lizbeth said, and the edge on her voice startled her. It had started like that with Vi, a shrill-edged voice, a flat defiance of anything that forced her from the comfortable trance she had dug for herself, a hiding place to dream of what might have been. "Don't worry," she repeated emphatically. "I plan to find other interests, but I'm not sure God wants me to ignore Kent and Jo altogether."

Vi laughed—brittle laughter. "So? And it's what God wants you to do? Don't let Charley hear you talk like that. Kent Wilson caused Cecil to die and we're not forgetting it."

"But we agreed long ago that Cecil's with God," Lizbeth persisted patiently, following the argument she had rehearsed with Vi a thousand times.

"Cecil's with God, I know that," Vi said, quiet hot tears reddening and swelling her eyes. "I tell Charley he's all right with God. But he ties me to the bed at night and he says I better keep quiet about where Cecil is or they'll haul me off to the state hospital."

Again Lizbeth weighed Vi's words. Charley treated Vi tenderly as a child and never once had he mentioned what everyone believed would be the ultimate outcome, that she would undoubtedly be committed to a mental institution if she did not get better soon. The only mistake Lizbeth could discern in Charley's care of her was his refusal to accept Cecil's death as God's will. Until he did, Vi would not. Since their marriage, when she was seventeen, it was a known fact that Vi had never made a decision without Charley's aid.

"I suppose you know what they say about his wife?" Lizbeth said. "They say she doesn't believe in God. She made that statement herself."

"Matches him," Vi said, her gray eyes dull and hard. "He goes snatching and taking, snatching and taking."

Lizbeth sighed, thinking of the unutterable mystery of the mind. Even though Vi shook her head in a markedly insane fashion, she could analyze character astutely. "I'm afraid all of us are guilty of some snatching and taking," Lizbeth said. "I know I have my own shortcomings. That's why I think it's good to have a revival of God's Spirit in our hearts. Even the best Christian needs it."

"You're not going to the tent meeting, are you?" she asked. "Charley says I can't go."

Lizbeth knew well what Charley would say, but this was the primary reason for her visit. "I plan to go," she said. "That is, if you and Mr. Shedd will come to sit with Mother. At least one night."

"Well." Vi sat, sullenly staring at Lizbeth. "Well, you better learn to listen to old heads, young lady. Charley says preachers, coming in from the outside, are up to no good. What do these claim to be?"

"You mean what denomination?" Lizbeth asked. "I haven't heard anyone say. Evangelism should reach above denominational lines, don't you think?"

Vi started to reply but she stopped when Charley came into the kitchen, proudly holding a string of brook trout. "So Lizbeth's here," he said, pleased. "You'll have to stay for supper, Lizbeth. I cleaned the fish outside and it won't take long to cook them."

"Thanks," Lizbeth said. "I'd like to stay but Mother's by herself."

"Yes." He knew without being told. Lizbeth's life was a string of jerks and knots. Jerked from the bus station to the house, caring for her invalid mother. Unconscious of her clenched fists and a taut spinal column, Lizbeth was sitting as though alerted for a sudden departure. If Cecil had lived, her life would have been different, as would his own, and Vi's.

"I wish sometime you'd arrange to come for supper, or for lunch" he said. "Arrange it with Ina."

"I'd really like to and I will," Lizbeth promised. "But now I've come to arrange with you and Mrs. Shedd to sit with Mother so I can attend the tent revival one night."

He glared at her, perplexed that she continued in her devotion to an imagined God of love. He thought, If there is a God, He is a God of wrath, not of love. Show me consistently a God of wrath and in time I might accept that kind of God, but all the preachers on the face of the earth cannot persuade me to honor a God who is good and cruel at the same time.

Remembering then that he had no right to dictate her life, Charley asked bluntly, "Must you go? When do you want us?"

"What about Monday night?" she asked. Sunday night she would attend First Church, as she did routinely. "It's asking a great deal but if you can come then, I'd be much obliged."

"Think nothing of it," he said. "We'll come every night if you want us. But you couldn't hog-tie me and get me to that tent. I've seen too much hypocrisy from these traveling preachers."

"I couldn't possibly ask so much of you and Mrs. Shedd," she told him quietly, aggrieved that such a fine voice for whistling and singing old mountain ballads had never been lifted in thanksgiving and praise to God. "Vi needs a lot of rest, just as Mother does. But you'll never know how much I appreciate your help."

"You go and enjoy yourself but don't come bringing the preacher to talk me into joining the church," he warned. "I've had all I can stand of that."

Lizbeth glanced at Mrs. Shedd, nodding in sleep, her head lolling on the chair back. "She's asleep,"

Lizbeth said. "Has she been sleeping at night lately?"

"Not good," he answered, in a low uneasy voice. "When she sleeps she grieves about Cecil. She calls his name, over and over."

"It's so sad," she said. "If only—" She started to say if only he would accept Cecil's death as God's will. But Lizbeth chose the times carefully when she talked to Charley Shedd about God, and yet she had promised not to let him rest until he became a Christian. "If only she could get better," Lizbeth said. "Maybe a visit with Mother will help."

She arose then and bade him good-night. "Give my love to Mrs. Shedd and tell her I had to hurry on home." He promised, but he would promise anything that did not concern his spiritual welfare.

At the top of the hill, overlooking the valley town, she saw the lighted campground where workers were setting up tents for revival, scheduled to begin a week from Saturday. If she had the nerve, she would invite Kent and his wife to the revival. Yet they were sure to know that the tent was going up. She decided to say nothing about the tent revival, nor about the churches of Loganville. Kent could introduce her to his church. She would leave their souls to themselves, and to God. Or to whom it might concern.

      o   o   o

Resting her head against a pillow on the chair back, Mrs. Lambert had dropped off to sleep, as she often did when alone. Moriah, the big gray-striped cat, sat watchfully at the bedside table, purring lazily.

The cat slept when she slept but both awoke when Lizbeth came in at nine o'clock that night, her four broken shifts completed. Ready for any "news," Mrs. Lambert sat forward, her face pale with illness, yet alert and pleasant. She asked questions about the townspeople, a daily routine which made life bearable, and Lizbeth answered patiently, volunteering the humorous and unusual events of her day at the bus station, including talk of a bridal shower for Kent's new wife.

"But they don't need a thing for that house," Mrs. Lambert said rebukingly. "They don't need anything money can buy. You should give them your little white Bible, Lizbeth."

"I don't see how I can part with it. It was the last gift I received from Dad."

"Ashton would bless you for it," Mrs. Lambert said with quiet resolution. "He spent a lifetime trying to make others see God as he saw Him. You have plenty of Bibles and Testaments to spare. I'd give Jo the new one and let her and Kent put their own fingerprints on it."

"A Bible is probably the last thing in the world they want," Lizbeth said, taking off her shoes and resting her feet on the cool linoleum. "They say Jo plans to give a housewarming party soon after the shower. It will be announced in *The Loganville Weekly*. Everybody is invited. She's already planning her dress, so they say. Well, you see, I'm getting to be quite a gossip."

"Aren't we all?" Mrs. Lambert said and smiled wryly. "Let me tell you what Mrs. Mackey told

Ruth Webb. Ruth stopped in to see me an hour ago. May the Lord help us all, Kent's wife is an atheist."

When Lizbeth did not reply, she persisted, "Did you hear me, Lizbeth? Kent's wife doesn't believe in God. That's why I think you should give her the Bible."

All this Lizbeth knew already. At the bus station news came to the top, the new cream, and usually she was first to learn, not only of local occurrences but countywide, and often statewide, at first hand.

"Kent will have to teach her to believe in God," she said. This strange marriage did not concern her. Cecil had been taken from her and neither anger nor love could return him—laughing, full of zest, whole. Although she had not forgiven Kent, she controlled her anger publicly, and nothing more should be expected of her. Acting of his own free will, Kent had married a strange woman. This was his responsibility.

"Mrs. Mackey scolded Jo for talking so boldly," her mother pursued. "She told her if she hadn't admitted it, nobody would've known she was pagan."

"I don't question that," Lizbeth answered. "Unless you shock people as Jo did, nobody stops to wonder who is pagan and who is Christian. You can't tell the difference in most cases."

Mrs. Lambert sat silent a moment, her face showing pain. "It's not the Way," she said and Lizbeth realized that her mother was a Christian for whom there was a Way to live, the only Way, and it started with a capital letter.

34

"So many things are not the Way," Lizbeth said.

It was not the Way for her not to care how Kent and his wife managed their lives—and their souls. It was not the Way but she could not help feeling as she did. Not her grave but Cecil's—this was the grave Kent walked on, and it had twisted her heart beyond repair.

4

☐ AUGUST ON THE COAST or August in the mountains, it was practically the same, Jo thought, as she drove the station wagon, purchased for household uses, into the driveway. She stood a while once again gazing at the imposing Wilson house, the fresh white of its massive brick walls, resplendent in the scorching noonday sun.

"A bargain!" she exclaimed, smiling at the magnificence of the house. I got a bargain when I married Kent, she thought. Wait till we wake the town with our housewarming. Then everybody will have a tiny idea of Kent's wealth.

Standing where she parked the station wagon, near the kitchen door, she had a bird's-eye view of the Wilson possessions. The twenty-room house, the most prominent centennial mark in Kensington County, centered the broad grassy acres rolling toward the quiet Ocmaha River, half the merchants' houses in Loganville, six hundred acres of forest land—she stopped there.

Their first day here Kent had given her a résumé of his holdings. She had seen the pride on his handsome profile as he said, "That is mine; I built it," or "Father left that to me and it hasn't been changed." He had retained his serious intent until he left the business section, and circled the woodland, going toward Mrs. Baxley's house. In banter he remarked, "They say here my family imprinted its name on every broomstraw in the Wilson Woods. That's a thing you'll have to live with, my darling. A sprinkling of jealousy, a great deal of envy. And some hatred."

She smiled now, recalling the ride their first night here. Driving slowly in the moonlight, warm in Kent's love and in his proud possession of her, it had not mattered that he labeled her another "Wilson holding." Nor did it matter now. I married above myself and that's what every girl dreams of doing, she thought.

But there was a restlessness in her, a vague emptiness. And she recalled the short visit only hours before when they had stopped at the Baxleys. In reply to Jo's statement that she absolutely believed nothing about God, Sally Baxley had said, "Cole and Sadie would rise up in their graves if they could hear Kent's wife say a thing like that."

Shrugging the memory aside, she started into the

house, anxious to get an early afternoon start on the knee-length chiffon dress she was making for her initial party. It was midnight black and gossamer thin and enchanting.

At the water-soaked doorsteps, hewed from cherry wood when Kent's grandfather had built the house one hundred and two years ago, she picked up a late-winging July fly, dead of a wound received in flight. Probably it had driven hard through the gnarled oak treetops and had jammed itself against the house. Picking it up, she examined the wings—pure webbed lace, lovelier than anything Kent's money could purchase. The thought came and went, adding yet more to the gnawing uneasiness within her.

Who had the ingenuity to attach such beautiful wings to a mere insect? But, of course, it was a product of evolution, like herself, like Kent. At one time their ancestors were probably apes and the July fly might easily have been first cousin to the belfry bat. When she had told Kent that she wanted in the next life to be reincarnated into a thoroughbred race horse, he had become violently angry. She knew it was because the remark, alien to his senses, jarred him so intensely.

She went through the screened porch into the cool spacious kitchen and set the groceries on the table. Turning on the radio, she dialed her favorite jazz program broadcast from WAGV in Winterville. It was one of the few regional programs she did like. She avoided like the plague the numerous heart-rending sermons and it required dexterity not to get some of it mixed into her constant dialing, for Kent had never spoken a more blatant truth than when he said that Kensington County had produced more fanatics than Nazareth.

At that moment it occurred to her that since she believed nothing in the Bible and Kent had promised that he would not interfere with her avowed atheism, she might take down the religious symbols throughout the house.

She removed the embroidered hanging from the wall above the sink. It was actually the first thing she noticed when Kent brought her into the kitchen, following their arrival two weeks ago from the coast. From the convention in Preston, they had driven to the Atlantic for some time to become better acquainted before returning the two-hundred-mile journey to Loganville. The return had been a thing of dread for Kent, and this reluctance Jo still did not understand.

She examined the large high-walled room, called the Fire Room because here a log fire glowed on wintry days while the Wilsons entertained guests or read, or while Sadie sewed. And here Cole and Sadie had slept in the high roll-topped mahogany bed and here Kent had been born. It was the only part of the house not renovated seven years previously, when Kent came into full possession of the estate.

Only a month's time separated Kent's parents from earthly life into death, and this they would have liked, so Kent had told her, another thing she failed to understand. Who could ever be reconciled to death? Suddenly her green, wide-set eyes saw the black-lettered, GOD BLESS OUR HOME motto.

For all her love for him, Jo hated Kent's background, the countless "God bless" placards, the yellowed pages of old Bibles and religious periodicals, apt to fall from any shelf upon approach. Except for Kent, the part of him which she did love, she disliked Loganville and all its stuffy littleness.

But Kent will change, she thought now. If he doesn't get better, he will get worse, and I understand enough about the Christian religion to know it atrophies if not activated.

Forgetting the groceries purchased at the shopping center on the Johnston highway, she took the inscription from the wall and placed it in a laundry basket. Going rapidly through the long sprawling house, she plucked Bibles, pictures, bookmarks, and old religious magazines addressed to Kent's grandmother, Martha Wilson. Soon the basket was heaped, like a cornucopia, except that cornucopias symbolized great riches and somehow its adherents managed to keep Christianity in a state of pitiful poverty. That was one reason why she wanted none of it. She had seen enough poverty.

Born into a seaman's family where each parent welcomed the long separations, the periods of absolute liberty from marital vows, she and her five brothers, all older than herself, had long since scattered from coast to coast. They had been slum children of Lowndes, a small seaport town, but they had had freedom. Their parents had not interfered with any decision, or lack of decision, but had remained neutral about choices of religion, friends, spouses, vocations. They each had moved swiftly above their circumstances, she to a marriage of wealth, her brothers to affluent business positions, and Jo believed her parents had acted wisely.

Yet lack of restriction also had its penalty, she knew. She remembered her father who died in middle age of an alcohol-yellowed liver, only six months before a disease that baffled a dozen doctors killed her mother. She pondered the word Dr. Wardlaw had used when discussing her mother's condition, shortly before she died a year ago—escape. "Desire to escape, to hide, has brought death. Sedatives— too many sedatives," he said, shaking his head wearily. "I won't say she was an addict but she hasn't been fully awake in years. She simply slept herself to death."

Forcing herself to forget her disordered past, Jo selected a linen closet back of the guest rooms as a receptacle for the religious objects. Without form or order, she dumped them on the floor.

Later when Kent came home for lunch, she told him about her morning's occupation. "I did it, but I was a little afraid you mightn't like it," she said.

"The house is yours," he replied, though a shadow darkened his face. There had been sorrow in his life, but he had discovered that being with Jo was medicine for his tired tormented mind. He wanted her here—and he wanted her happy. "Do with it as you like."

Jo's quick eyes sized up the big front room. The tall mahogany clock on the mantel, more than a hundred years old, now indicated twelve o'clock. It's noonday in our lives, she thought gravely. Then afternoon and evening and night with irrevocable certainty. The thought left a touch of gravity on her piquant face.

"What were you thinking?" he asked.

"I was thinking that life can be so short—too short," she answered. "Let's make merry. Let's make this ancient mothballed old house ring with the sounds of bitter-sweet pleasure."

Jo's pensive mood made Kent pause. Until the convention, hardly a month ago, he had not known her, not until she came with her employer, a merchant from a small factory town in North Carolina. She worked for him as his secretary but at the convention, in the presence of his competitors, he expected her to blossom. And she did—gay, beautiful, young, a virtuous pagan among literally dozens of office concubines who had variously compromised themselves for job, prestige, exclusive clothes, jewelry, furs, and countless other paltry reasons.

"Sure, we'll live it up," he finally promised. "Do with the house as you like."

She surveyed the roll-top mahogany bed where Kent had been born, in his parents' middle age, the only child of their forty-eight-year union. She noticed particularly the immaculate coverlid, tufted by Sadie Wilson's hands.

"She was a thrifty craftsman, I can see that," Jo said, admiring the beautiful meticulous needlework. "You've told me a lot about her, but what was she really like? Did she ever lose her temper as I do, or laugh or sing? Was she gay, Kent?"

He sighed. He had been fond of his mother, and

42

he had admired the industry of both parents. They had instructed him to restrict his conversation and his deeds to God's will and now he wondered if taking this pretty pagan as his wife had forfeited his inheritance to the heaven he had believed in. "I'll show you the family album when I have time," he volunteered.

She laughed, shrugging her shoulders. "You're only making excuses, I know more about you and your family than you think. Before our wedding, I discussed you fully with Dan Hambridge, your former classmate at State U."

"Oh," he said, raising his eyebrows. That conversation must have taken place before Dan, coming down from Cedar Lake, had left with his secretary. Disappeared would be a better word, since they did not reappear. "Oh," he repeated quietly, wondering what Dan would think of his wife, chosen from myriad secretaries attending the convention. If the opportunity presented itself, he would tell him that Jo came to him, virginally pure. A man wanted other men to know that he had chosen a virtuous wife. Say what they would about Jo's resolute paganism, they should know that no man had touched her before their wedding night.

"Tell me," she persisted. "What would your mother think of me?"

He did not answer at once, engrossed with the fact that Jo was literally without God. Any suggestion of taking religion to herself, except as a curious thing to discuss, she dismissed with a good-natured laugh. For all his own sins, for all his disloyalty to a rich religious heritage, he knew that Jehovah God was the only true living God.

He recalled that the Bible spoke of unequal yoking between a man and a woman. Regarding religion, he and Jo were far apart. She had only a smattering knowledge of the Bible while his Bible training had been thorough. Still he knew almost nothing about the actual nature of God.

Yet for better or for worse, he had loved Jo at first sight and after a three-day courtship, had married her. She was his wife. The Lamberts, the Shedds— he had regretted the grief he gave them. But his heart and soul now had turned completely to his wife.

And then, shrugging his shoulders, he answered her question: "If my mother could see you, she'd think you the loveliest girl in ten counties."

"But she was a Christian," she persisted. "Your friend told me that, too. Would she try to make a Christian of me?"

"I think so, but I promised to leave all that up to you," he answered decisively.

"I can't imagine myself conforming to that, the being good and turning the other cheek," she said. "Yet I wonder sometimes—about everything. You're so different. Every man I've ever met was looking for a girl just like his mother. I guess that's why I was courted by dozens but proposed to only by you."

"I loved you and I married you," he said curtly. "I intend for the people here to accept you as you are."

"But they already know I don't believe as you

do," she said. "There was a time when I tried to believe. But I can't. I've had my share of fun and I intend to keep on having fun—even in Loganville."

Abruptly he took her in his arms. "Listen, my dear, confessions are all right made to me, but nobody else needs to know everything you believe and don't believe."

Her face went white. Only yesterday she had told Mrs. Mackey, housekeeper at the Wilson house for the past thirty years, how she felt about the Wilsons' religious beliefs. She remembered the awed old face, withered but kind, with the eyelids lowered in an attempt not to offend her. It was the same with everyone in this town of fanatics. Except for his vow not to interfere with her relatives' persuasion, this included Kent.

45

5

□ A MONTH AFTER Kent brought his bride to Loganville, preparations got under way for a bridal shower. Women who envied Jo her rather casual, exceptional beauty and who ignored her ideas on religion grew excited over the coming event. Many had lost patience over the unusual delay, caused mainly by the community's reluctant acceptance of an alien to the church. The occasion would provide an opportunity to examine this gay attractive woman who promised to set a new pace in fashions and social customs. Women who feared her influence and were awed that she readily admitted to spiritual infidelity, also planned to come, bringing gifts as well as prayers for her salvation.

Among the latter was Lizbeth Lambert. She forced

46

herself to perform this current obligation and be done with the winsome stranger. The fourth Friday of August when the sun brought a scorching heat wave over the valley she decided to go to the town square to purchase an ice tea serving set.

"It's all I can think of on a sweltering day," she said, as she cleaned the sandwich table with a hot soapy sponge. She regretted disappointing Mrs. Lambert, but she simply could not offer the Bible as a shower gift.

"I'll finish your shift," Ina volunteered. "Take off and go home. You look pale as a rag doll."

"You don't have to say it twice," Lizbeth said, taking off her apron and straightening the skirt of her white uniform. "Are you sure you can handle the next rest stop?"

"Think nothing of it," she answered. "It's all for the cause."

"I've worried so long about what to give Jo Wilson." Lizbeth met Ina's glance and she admitted quickly, "It's a duty-gift, nothing more."

"Then why give it?" Ina asked. "Frankly, why be a hypocrite?"

Lizbeth considered several replies. A Christian had to do some unpleasant things. None were subject to more studied surveillance than a Christian. "I plan eventually to invite her to become a church member," she answered.

"What about Kent?" The question was intended as a rebuke, not for Kent's sake but for Lizbeth's. "You haven't spoken to him since Cecil died. Getting soft, huh?"

"I'll take care of that part somehow," Lizbeth answered, with a finality that forbade further questioning. "See you tomorrow, God willing."

"Yes. Let's hope so."

○　　○　　○

Lizbeth stopped at Murray's Family Shop first but finding nothing that seemed fitting, she went to the Pendleton Department Store. As she started in, Kent Wilson emerged. His puzzled frown changed instantly into a friendly smile when she impulsively said, "Hello."

He stopped, indubitably surprised. "It's Lizbeth," he said as he drew a long breath. "I'm glad to see you."

"Thanks."

"I'm sure you've heard I got married," he said, smiling. "I want you to meet Jo soon. I think you'll like her."

"I'm anxious to meet her," Lizbeth said. It was another duty. She should be perpetually eager to make contact with the unsaved, she knew. Not even Ina could find hypocrisy in this purpose.

"Then we'll see that you do," he answered, and lifting his hat, he went out.

This Jo, Lizbeth thought, as she sauntered down the aisle toward the rear counter.

Lizbeth had heard in essence that Jo was a feminine phenomenon. The tale that she was pagan had dwindled when the people saw her dazzling physical beauty and felt the warmth of her charming personality. They forgot the infidelity of old Mr. Crowley Sutton, living in seclusion on the mountain and curs-

48

ing God while dying. A beautiful pagan should not be compared to a vile old man who died without God, or so they apparently believed. And Lizbeth herself found it difficult to place Jo in the same category as the hard weathered inebriate to whom the townspeople referred as Old Crow. Yet they were both self-confessed unbelievers, lost without God.

She selected the best tea serving set available and while the purchase was being transacted she puzzled over the public demand to do the expected, however much the heart rebelled. Stopping at the candy shop she purchased a bag of popcorn for Ina's children, before hurrying on. As the sun slipped behind a cloud the air became decidedly cooler, riffling through dry leaves, stirring up a scent of early autumn. Old Brass Bald looked gloomy, lying like a slope-headed monster beneath the dark clouds. Everybody and everything is angry at something or somebody these days, she thought.

Then she remembered her own attitude, her daily battle to control her resentment for Kent Wilson. She wondered whether a part of her heart could abscess and the other part remain whole. When she reached the mailbox at the hedgerow, Kent and Jo passed, sitting close together, talking intently.

God have mercy on me, she prayed silently. I fairly despise those two people. I'll have to admit it. The hatred in my heart can no longer be sealed up. She waited a moment for reassurance but there was none. The sense of oppression from the day's weather and her own defeat went with her as she entered the house.

Next morning she felt the need for a long talk with her mother before starting the day's shift. On the kitchen table she kept a small loaf-like container. By lifting the lid she had access to dozens of Bible verses, printed on slick paper. This morning she drew Jeremiah 33:3 and read aloud: "Call unto me, and I will answer thee, and shew thee great and mighty things, which thou knowest not."

Replacing the tiny card she turned to Mrs. Lambert. "If I only knew what to ask for. So much needs doing but I'm really only running around in circles." Then she grasped her mother's old hands and smiled with more cheer than she felt. "But I shouldn't worry you. You must get tired sitting here all day long looking out the window."

"What if I do get tired sitting here all day long looking out the window?" Mrs. Lambert scolded reprovingly. "It's nothing compared to the world full of sinful children God has to worry over."

"I hadn't thought of it like that," Lizbeth said. "I guess it takes being a mother to understand how a parent feels. And God is the Father of so very many."

"The obedient and the disobedient," she said. "I'm sure, like any parent, He spends more time grieving over His unruly than He rejoices over His good children."

The unruly, Lizbeth thought. The Kents and the Jos—who admire nobody in this world more than the Kents and the Jos.

On Saturday *The Loganville Weekly* announced

that Jo's bridal shower would take place at Florrie's
Beauty Shoppe on the first Saturday afternoon of
September. It was a compromise between a private
home and the church basement. More than a dozen
town matrons had offered their houses for the occasion and twice as many had voted for the church
basement. Occasionally events were held in the rec-
reation hall, but many frowned upon Kent taking
an unchurched wife and the basement vote was over-
ruled.

When Florrie Woods, a buxom blond beautician
with a twenty-year practice to her credit, set her
head about an idea, it was carried out. It surprised
no one then when the weekly community paper, in
a front-page spread, announced that the gift shower,
to which the public was invited, would be an open
house reception.

Ina brought a copy of the newspaper to the bus
station when she reported for work at ten o'clock.
"If you live long enough, you'll see everything,"
she told Lizbeth. "Loganville will have her blue bloods
yet. See here."

Lizbeth stopped refilling the sugar jars and read
the news article. "Kent owns *The Loganville Weekly*," she said. "He can publish what he wishes, I
think."

"Pity the poor creatures who have to live here,"
Ina said. "From now on it will be a weekly journal
on Jo's doings."

Lizbeth suddenly felt vague about what God wanted
her to do. Even though she had tried to give Him
her full life since she lost Cecil, God had not di-

rected her with a clear-cut purpose.

"I'm mixed up," she murmured as she stamped a seventy-nine-cent ticket to Johnston. "I don't know what to do. Maybe God doesn't need someone like me, someone walking around without a heart." She would admit to any that her heart lay buried with Cecil, in his lonely grave on the hill in the cemetery back of the church.

That night when Lizbeth started to leave, having finished her four split shifts, Ina apologized for having spoken so bluntly regarding Jo. "I'm sorry," she said penitently. "It's the truth, though. Imagine a bridal shower for someone like that! I'll bet she'll hoot when she sees the cheap little presents people will bring."

Lizbeth laughed. "I was careful not to remove the label on my tea set," she said. " 'Pendleton Department Store.' How does that sound?"

"Not much better," she answered, brutally frank. "Loganville is simply Loganville. Everything and everyone here is marked 'Loganville.' That's why big Kent brought back an import. People here only pretend to be shocked at her. They actually wish they could be her."

Lizbeth nodded. She herself had secretly wished she had hair with a dark sheen like Jo's, that she had bell-tone laughter, that she had not been five-feet-eight inches tall but a petite four-feet-eleven like Jo. "You're a seer," Lizbeth said. "You sort things out so quickly."

"No, it isn't altogether what I see that makes me different," she answered. "I just say what I think."

Lizbeth pondered Ina's remarks as she walked home a little later. The truth, bitter as gall, had stung. Kent had indirectly spoiled her life and she truly despised him but she kept it secret. But must she go on all her days, quietly resentful, hardly knowing which way to turn? She had never known how to conduct herself in regard to Kent and now that he had a wife, it had become even more tedious. Soon Jo would know about Cecil. Would she pity Lizbeth or would she despise her, in the poverty of her broken, twisted heart?

o   o   o

The current issue of *The Loganville Weekly* devoted to the bridal shower only a small back-page corner, stating that fifty-three guests called at Florrie's Beauty Shoppe with gifts for the radiant bride, who wore a gentian blue dress and a tiny corsage of white roses. When Lizbeth read it, she could hardly believe the reporter spoke of the same event she had attended the preceding night. Fifty-three was the exact guest count, of course, but they came in fifty-three different disguises.

Some were jealous, many envious. Others looked disapprovingly at one who dared defy the God of their heritage. All brought packages but each gift bore a marked resemblance to the giver. Some were purchased with the hope of impressing the recipient, others with a sense of social duty, expecting subtle reimbursement. Lizbeth's own was merely a performance of duty and for that attitude she would forever feel ashamed. Jo had opened it, looked at it briefly. And smiling, she nodded toward Lizbeth. Then she pushed it aside beneath a mountain of tissue paper, and proceeded to open the other presents.

When all the gifts were unwrapped and admired, when dozens of guests witnessed the ingenuity of each giver with soft feminine "ohs" and "ahs" Maurine Dickson said, "Isn't Jo the lucky one? She got her man and what a man!"

"Yes, I am lucky, very lucky," Jo agreed solemnly. "I do have a wonderful husband. He lets me have my way about everything."

ON MONDAY NIGHT, as they promised, Charley and Vi came to sit with Mrs. Lambert. Lizbeth brought a tray of iced tea, fruit, and cakes and made them comfortable. "My three favorite people," she said, bidding them good-bye.

"You be careful," Charley cautioned. "It's better to walk than to get in the car with strangers."

"I'll be careful," she promised. She left them, quietly, strangely unstirred, not filled with the usual elation that accompanied her attendance at revival meetings.

The campground was located a quarter mile from the Lambert house. Every house on Elm Street was lighted brightly and being acquainted with someone in each household, she knew that very few people would attend the tent revival. They went to First Church, or to one of the other two denominational churches, if they went anywhere. Most of the members believed that religious tent gatherings belonged to the ignorant and the emotional.

As she approached the Caswell house, she heard loud voices, a shout, an obscenity, a brief silence, and a woman weeping. The Caswells' marriage had been stormy since the beginning when Wyatt brought his bride from Roopville five years ago. There was little hope of improvement so long as he spent his time at Paw's Place, Lizbeth feared.

Then there was the Wilson house, topping the hill above the river crossing, every window lighted. Were they terribly happy in that house? Did they know the ecstatic love she had dreamed of sharing with Cecil? She believed they had in abundance all that she had been denied and for a moment she hated them. Then her disciplined mind rejected the thought.

"Father, for this reason, because of that very household, my heart is not right," she said. "Forgive me and take this burden from me, if it be Thy will. Amen." She walked on, looking neither to the right nor to the left to avoid glimpses behind curtained windows of other homes beaming with a certain glow that Lizbeth believed she would never know.

      °   °   °

Though the tent was full when she arrived, Lizbeth found a seat near the front. She faced the speaker's improvised rostrum, and the masses of home-grown flowers flanking it. She knew that not one flower

brought for the beautification of the altar went un-
noted by the Lord God.

Listening to the organ's slow chords, waiting for
the evangelist to appear, she recalled the twenty-
sixth chapter of Exodus in which God had designated
the exact yardage and selvage for decorating the
tabernacle. She regretted that she had not brought
a bouquet of zinnias and marigolds for this altar.

Finally the volunteer choir appeared, followed by
the evangelist, a tall wiry red-haired man who did
not look impressive. Lizbeth saw at once that his
face was serene and open. He carried himself quietly
but with an innate assurance. Yet Lizbeth felt disappointment. She had expected—what had she expected? She did not know, but not this one.

As he opened the Bible to read, she noticed a
gold wedding band on his third finger. He would
be married, of course, but she could not discern the
least aura of romance about this man who appeared
to have no thought other than to serve at the altar
of God.

He read the sixth chapter of Hosea and then he
repeated the fourth verse: "O Ephraim, what shall
I do unto thee? O Judah, what shall I do unto thee?
for your goodness is as a morning cloud, and as the
early dew it goeth away." For a still moment he
gazed at the congregation, his eyes fused, his eyebrows lifted, his entire face a question mark.

And then he started to preach. Gifted of tongue
and vocabulary, his face and hands mobile and ex-
pressive, he acted out his message. Cavalierly bowing
to mock invitations to sin and answering, hand over

heart, he said, "I consent! I consent to vice. I consent to confusion. I consent to degradation. I consent to put wealth and possessions before family love until all emotions between family members disintegrate. I consent to send my father and my mother, my sisters and my brothers, my husband, my wife, my child to hell because I cannot offend them by even suggesting that they should get their hearts right with God. I consent to havoc, to worldliness, to sin. I consent to murder."

He stood quietly for a while, then he whispered hoarsely, "You don't believe that? Why not? You can't tell a Christian from anyone else now. A true Christian practices self-discipline; he controls his desire for appetite and pleasure. Being a Christian is virtually the hardest task in the world. A Christian cannot keep the fact that he is a follower of Jesus a secret. Impossible thought! And when the world finds out about a Christian, look out, that person will work a hard row."

Concluding the service, the invitation was offered. Lizbeth watched the seekers after faith, the newly redeemed, walk the sawdust aisles along with Christians, reawakened to penitence and remorse. But she stood immovable and confused. How did one win a soul to God? Here they came, by one's, by two's, by dozens to the altar! She had not fulfilled her promise to a dying sweetheart that she would win his agnostic, rebellious father to God. Until she did, she knew there would be no light in her life, no song in her heart. Yet—how?

Later walking homeward, she admitted her own

guilt. She was daily consenting to murder by knowing God's statutes and not executing His orders. Her name "Elizabeth" meant consecrated to God. By remaining neutral while others floundered, she had consented to their lost condition. She agreed, in essence, not only to the murder of others but to the deterioration of her own soul. But first she must win Charley Shedd. Then she could think of others. As she walked into the yard of her home, she paused to look up at the Big Dipper tilted directly over Loganville. A cicada shrilled in monotone; a mockingbird sang his repertoire from the sweet bay tree. Wrapped in the wonder of it all, she stood in the stillness, breathing the fragrant night air. Then and there it came to her ears inwardly, or perhaps it was spoken to her soul, she did not know exactly; but she knew without a doubt that God had commanded: "Win Jo."

In dismay she recognized it as an order, and she knew from whence it came. Yet she could not answer. If only Jo were someone else!

There was Mr. Shedd to consider. Her promise to Cecil had been a promise to God as well. She could not understand the wisdom of winning Jo at the risk of losing all influence over Mr. Shedd's possible conversion.

Yet it was true what the preacher had said. Generally speaking, one could not tell a Christian from any other in Loganville. The whole community had closed its eyes to evil and the signs of evil. Few seemed to care who were saved and who were lost, and few were concerned enough to learn the truth.

Many had adopted the broad plan for tolerance: live and let live. God, in His great mercy, will not exact from anyone eternal suffering in hell. If there's a heaven, there's a purgatory, a sort of prep school, for the naughty to get a little pre-training for heaven.

When did such a ridiculous philosophy take root, even in remote mountain towns like Loganville, Lizbeth wondered. And then, stricken with the knowledge that people all about her were being eternally lost, she answered, "I'll try to win Jo."

A peace settled within her and she knew that God had accepted her answer. She went inside then, silently acknowledging that she could not understand the ways of God. The majesty of His dealing filled her with awe.

"Was it a good meeting?" Mrs. Lambert asked, propping herself on three fat feather pillows, ready for a long talk. "I sent Charley and Vi on home a little early. Vi was getting sleepy and we saw the cars coming from the campground. I knew you'd be on directly."

"Yes, it was a good meeting, Mother. There were dozens who found Christ and many Christians too that rededicated their lives to God."

"What about you, dear?" she asked, stroking Moriah's head gently, warmed by her soft purring. "What did the meeting give you?"

"I made a decision tonight. I'll give my little white Bible to Jo, as you suggested. You're so wise and good. I hope to win her to Christ, but I know it's too big a job for me."

"The Lord never gives anybody a job He considers too big for that person to shoulder," Mrs. Lambert said. "Your father would be happy if he were here tonight."

"Yes, I know," Lizbeth said, still feeling the weight of her new burden—the conversion of Jo Wilson to Christianity.

7

□ LIZBETH spent a sleepless night thinking of Jo. That she would come to God finally Lizbeth had no doubt. God had commanded and the order must be fulfilled.

But how? A war general mapped his strategy—designing, calculating, and utilizing the utmost wisdom. In this project she too must plan with care. Craftily enough to gain Jo's attention, calculating enough that if she failed, it would be marked as her own failure, and not God's.

When dawn came, lighting the pineland with pastel shadings, Lizbeth knew that she could not handle the job single-handedly. She would go to the Baxleys' house, near the campground, where the Reverend Neal Redmond was staying during the revival. She would confide in him her difficulty and her need and seek his counsel.

At noon Lizbeth dialed the Baxley residence and the Reverend Redmond answered. She knew that his host, elderly Jethro Baxley, had made his rambling twelve-room house a station for any who wished to contact the evangelist. Lizbeth was not surprised when the Reverend Redmond answered.

"This is Lizbeth Lambert," she said. "I need advice about something very important and I wonder whether I could see you sometime today."

"Yes, certainly, Miss Lambert," he answered. "I'll be glad to help you, if I can."

She explained that she had a two-hour break in the afternoon. "I'd like to talk with you in confidence," she said. "I could meet you there or at my own home."

"Fine. Then why not come on over here?" he invited.

"I'll leave the bus station at two o'clock then," she said.

"I'll be here," he promised.

Two hours later, sitting in the high-ceilinged living room at the Baxleys', Lizbeth had a moment of wishing to retreat. But the keen blue eyes, widened by zeal when she mentioned that she had come about someone lost without God, held her to the finish. He demanded all the details and watched her as she talked, occasionally nodding his head. The receding line of wavy red hair, gray at the temples, showed that life had taken a sizable toll during his thirty-two years.

"I'd never have volunteered for this," she confided, when she finished with the pertinent details. "You can see how it is. Kent and Jo are happy with each other and maybe Kent is a little penitent about Cecil, but I don't think he understands how I feel."

"But if Jo needs you, and if God needs you to work with Jo, I believe you have no choice," he said quietly.

She sat silent for a while. This man had a depth and a width that amazed her. No Cecil, who laughed so readily that one remembered him as laughing all the time. No Kent, so bottled up with reserve that none understood him. But here was a man of sterling, and she felt confident in his counsel. She could not imagine him in the role of husband and yet he wore a thin gold wedding band.

"Then you think I should seek out Jo?" she asked.

"Yes, and her husband too. Go to Kent and tell him you've forgiven him. Witness to him about your faith in God. We don't know—perhaps he needs help as much as Jo."

"I hardly know Jo," she said. "Except for Kent, she would be like anyone else I've witnessed to." Like the bus drivers, like countless transients in the station, like the young people at her church. "But when I think of Kent I feel a turbulence I can't describe."

He nodded. "I think I know," he said. "Not even God Himself can force you to forgive Kent, but if you wish to win Jo to the Lord, your own heart must be made right first. Created anew."

"Then I have some more thinking to do," she

said. She arose and started out, but he stopped her.

"I've a snapshot I want you to see," he said, opening his billfold. "This is my wife and our two daughters. The children were three and one when it was made two years ago."

"Oh, what a happy pose," she said. The girls in ruffled white dresses sitting close to their mother, the father bending attentively over his family, presented a typically wholesome Christian family.

"I wanted you to see my family when we were together," he said. "Then maybe you can understand your own situation better. A month after this picture was made our girls were burned to death in an apartment house fire. We left them there while we conducted a revival in another town. My wife never knew an easy moment thereafter. She died quite suddenly one night . . . stricken and gone before the ambulance reached the hospital."

"I'm sorry," she murmured. "So very sorry. Please forget all I've said about myself."

"I will, on condition," he promised. "Forget yourself, for our Lord's sake, then get busy and carry out His direct command. This way, I assure you, will lead to happiness."

"Not to marital happiness," she said. "I can never love anyone else. My heart died with Cecil."

He turned away briefly, then he faced her again, his blue eyes significantly piercing. "No one could possibly understand better than I," he said. "But the kingdom of God can't wait out a long siege of self-pity."

Startled, she repeated, "Self-pity?"

"Yes. We all have self-pity to some extent, but it blights a Christian witness as perhaps nothing else in this world."

"Yes," she said dazedly. "Yes, I can see it would."

She left then, quietly determined that in whatever circumstances she found herself she must remember his counsel. Winning a soul to God was war—total war—and a true soldier possessed the remarkable facility of selflessness. That truth had been indelibly imprinted on her mind and she had learned it in the deep intensity of the saddest, bluest eyes she had ever seen.

8

□ LOGANVILLE CITIZENS called Kent a "business genius." At the merchants' conventions he was known to be a money-making wizard. Yet Kent, not aspiring to titles, looked only for the reward of effort which to him meant money. He got out early, before the town fully awakened. The lights went on at the Wilson house at 4:30 each morning. And though Jo balked and yawned, out of love, and from the wisdom of comparing her former life with her present, she rose to make his breakfast.

On Tuesday morning, after Lizbeth received her conviction to win Jo, Kent opened his clothing store at six o'clock, not an unusual hour for him. Frequently he opened early to go over the books and to personally check the inventory. This morning he noticed the hour by his wrist watch and he raised an eyebrow when he saw Lizbeth going up the woods path toward his home.

He wondered what message she carried. In the past she had visited his mother, asking for old copies of religious magazines or wanting to check something by his grandmother's ancient Bible. But that was before Cecil died, before the full blame for his death had been placed on Kent's shoulders. He watched her until she disappeared behind the pine grove.

He smiled half in contempt, half in anger, for he knew well that she had started her campaign to convert his wife. He would forbid it if he thought for a moment that it would bother Jo. Still it could be a good friendship . . . it could, he mused. Perhaps in this manner and by this token the Shedds had relented in their hatred toward him. If Lizbeth actually were no longer against him, it would add to his peace of mind—and undoubtedly to his success in this rapidly secular town.

Kent knew hatred firsthand. Since he was twenty, when the train-car crash occurred at the river crossing, killing Cecil and paralyzing the whole town with grief, he had felt the icy thrust of hatred. If by some miracle this burden could be removed, then his life could be counted as near perfect, insofar as personal contentment was concerned.

Going inside, he went from counter to counter, checking merchandise, jotting notes on a small pad. While others slept he worked with greatest care and while they waked they envied him his goods. He examined a boy's suit that had been marked down without his specific order and he made a note to check on the clerk—probably Frank Linton—when he came in at 8:30. If he could not teach his employees the love of diligent service, then he would enforce diligence at any cost.

           o   o   o

Lizbeth's legs trembled. Her heart fluttered like bottled insect wings. But she knocked at the Wilsons' front door. Though she knew Jo was in the kitchen, or some part of the rooms at the rear, local custom bade her enter at the front door on a first visit, implying importance to the visitor rather than the household.

Promptly soft-slippered steps sounded down the hall and the door opened. A velvet ribbon in her hair matched her rose-printed morning coat. She looked at first glance altogether unselfconscious and at ease. But there was more in her manner—an awareness of her position as mistress of this great old house and as wife of Loganville's richest man. Raising her brow ever so slightly when she saw Lizbeth, Jo realized that she must learn to accept Kent's people. And she knew the ways of the common people far better than Kent would ever know them. She had been one of them, the poorest of the poor.

"Miss Lizbeth Lambert?" It was both question and statement. Lizbeth nodded, smiling, showing two rows of well-kept teeth that had never been brilliant as were Jo's. She apologized for her early morning visit, explaining her times of working.

Jo smiled graciously. "Do come in. I've been up early and I'd love company over a second cup of coffee." 69

She is adorable, Lizbeth thought. Nobody can blame Kent for marrying her.

Jo led the way to the breakfast nook, the red booths cozily inviting. Red-checked cotton cloths and matching napkins graced the table, built by Kent only a year ago. When he remodeled the house, mixing the old with the modern, it was assumed that he planned to marry but it developed that he intended to do so only when he found a girl who suited him. This girl matched him and no doubt he would resent any effort by anyone to change her, Lizbeth mused.

Jo poured two cups of coffee, then excusing herself, she disappeared into the kitchen. Within minutes she reappeared with a plate of brown toast and little sausage biscuits. "It's your first visit and you must have breakfast with me," she said. She sat down opposite Lizbeth and then added pleasantly, "Now we can talk. You have something you must tell me before you start work at the bus station?"

Did God, in all His wisdom, consider what a task He had assigned her? Did He understand how every nerve in her body quaked when she remembered His command: "Win Jo"? I'll have to talk to Kent, I'll have to forgive him, Lizbeth thought, and she sighed so that Jo's eyebrows shot up and she asked the question first with her restrained smile, following it verbally: "So? It's that bad?"

Lizbeth smiled. "No, it's wonderful," she answered. "I came for several reasons. I wanted to talk to you, but Mother believed I should have given you a Bible instead of the tea serving set. So I brought

70

the Bible Dad gave me his last Christmas with us."
She handed the package to Jo and watched as she
took it from the box, delighted that it was a sur-
prise-gift, whatever it might be.

"A place for weddings, births, and deaths," she
observed as she leafed through briefly. "We're married and we hope there will be births, many of
them, but perish the thought of death. So this is
a useful gift. Maybe our grandchildren will refer to
this book when they apply for the family's coat of
arms."

Trying to interest her in the salvation plan was
like pouring a glass of water on the Ocmaha River,
Lizbeth knew at once, but unflaggingly persistent,
she said, "It's good for reading, too. You'll be surprised when you start reading."

Jo shrugged her shoulders. "I don't know whether
I'll read it, but I do appreciate you and your mother
thinking of me," she said, stirring sugar in her coffee.
"Kent told me your mother was a wheelchair invalid."

"Yes, I'd like you to meet her sometime," Lizbeth
said. After an interval of casual community talk, she
departed, promising to return to Jo's housewarming
party.

∘   ∘   ∘

Lizbeth reached the bus station at opening time
just when a Greymount bus backed into the parking
lot. Thus began the morning, the address system
busy with announcements of incoming and outgoing
buses. At ten o'clock when Ina reported to work,
Lizbeth went immediately to Kent's office at the

71

Wilson Clothing Store.

He did not appear surprised to see her. When he watched her walking to his house early that morning, he knew that he could expect further developments. "Well, Lizbeth," he said, in the same manner as Jo had greeted her. "Please be seated."

She took the chair across from his desk and without preliminaries, said, "I've been to visit your wife, Kent. She invited me to have breakfast with her, and I did. I must say you married a gracious lady."

"Yes." He waited, clasping and unclasping his hands, intermittently twisting the gold wedding band, as though trying to make it fit.

"I hope she will become a Christian," she said. "I hope in time she'll understand the Christian faith and life. And I hope that I can help her. But before I do anything more, I wanted to tell you I've forgiven you."

"Forgiven me?" His eyes opened wide, staring at her. "I think you refer to Cecil's accident?"

"Yes," she answered. "I have only today forgiven you, since I talked with Jo."

"She asked you to forgive me?" he said. "You told her all you knew about me?"

"We didn't mention you," she answered, recalling with wonder that the master of that vast house had not been brought into the conversation, nor given much thought at all. "You may tell her I came to your office if you wish. She knows nothing about it. I came because I had to tell you I no longer hate you."

He remained silent a while, then he said, "Thank

you. While we're on the subject, it's quite all right with me for you to talk to Jo about the Christian faith but please leave my name out of it. Need I say more? Just leave me out of it."

She arose then and he stood, too, leaning a little toward her, protectively, ever the gentleman. "Thanks for talking to me," she said as she turned to go. "You needn't worry about yourself—not in regard to Jo. Good-bye."

She started back to the bus station but at the corner of Elm and Banks Street, she met Charley Shedd. His long eager stride led toward the pool hall and the color in his ruddy face heightened when he saw her, knowing she surmised his intentions.

"I saw you coming from the Wilson Store," he said, after bidding her good morning. "Patronizing the business now?"

"No, I didn't make any purchases." Long ago they had agreed to avoid Kent's store and she had pleaded with him to have nothing to do with Paw's Place. It was a sort of exchange agreement. "I talked with Kent," she confessed.

He was clearly stunned. "What about, if you don't mind telling?"

"I don't mind at all," she said. "I told him I'd forgiven him about Cecil. I had to do it. Earlier this morning I went to see Jo."

Charley's breathing grew violent. "The tent meeting did it," he exploded.

"No, Mr. Shedd, God did it. Last night I realized I'd been giving only a small part of my life to Him. Now I must witness, heart, soul, and body. Giving all, expecting nothing back."

"That beats all," he spluttered. "I'm sorry now Vi and I sat with Martha. The tent meeting made you lose your head. Kent's kind—and his wife's kind —can't be helped."

"I know how you feel, Mr. Shedd, but I can't do otherwise," Lizbeth said. "They need help. All people without God need guidance."

"If I could believe at all, I would believe," he said. "But how can I believe in a God who allows such awful things to happen? They talk about how powerful He is. I tell you, I can't make sense of it."

None knew better than Lizbeth that God's ways are mysterious, but she did not argue. "Someday we'll understand," she said, quoting Cecil. "Everything will be all right." Even as she said it, she doubted it. How could everything be right again? Could God return Cecil to her whole, a laughing lighthearted young man, unpredictable as the stars, but lovably so?

She had no answer, but when she went up the low cement steps into the Lambert yard, wind-swept and barren, she thought, "My life is barren, like the yard. All I ever wanted has been taken away from me." And without a moment's hesitation, fired with new zeal, she promised, " 'Though he slay me, yet will I trust in him.' "

9

□ "I'LL HAVE TO SPEAK to Jo again, sort of a follow up to my visit," she told Mrs. Lambert that night after supper as they sat on the porch, watching the summer constellations shift across the southern sky. Lizbeth had conscripted Mrs. Lambert's help. They had prayed together in hundreds of instances for various people in situations both crucial and mundane. But they had directed much of their effort in Jo's direction. "Maybe next week I'll have more time."

"That's the pity," Mrs. Lambert said regretfully. "Nobody has time now to snatch a soul from eternal torment."

"Not many take time, that's true," Lizbeth said. "I don't think many people care what happens to

75

others, so long as they and theirs are comfortable and happy."

Mrs. Lambert shook her head. "I remember a long time ago, we thought it a big joke when someone described a selfish man at prayer with the little rhyme, 'God bless me and my wife, and our son John and his wife. Us four and no more.' But now it seems no joke at all. It's good for families to cling together, but no family should exclude neighbors and friends. We can't overlook anyone who needs us and remain in favor with God."

Lizbeth went over and shook her gently. "Someday I'm going to have a gentleman-friend with a car come and we'll take you for a ride in the country," she said. "We'll not exclude you."

"Nothing would make me happier," she said, brightening. "If you could find a nice young man, you'd be much happier. But then I imagine he'd balk when he saw me."

"There you go again," Lizbeth said, laughing delightedly. "I'll bring a tray of lemonade and maybe that'll cheer you up."

"Temporarily it will," she answered. "You help me forget with lemonade; another gambles, another gets intoxicated, another races on the public—" She stopped abruptly. "Forgive me, dear. I didn't intend to remind you."

"You didn't remind me," Lizbeth answered firmly. "I'm conscious of how Cecil died every waking minute."

"Yes. Bring the lemonade, Lizbeth. Maybe after a while someone will come to visit."

They sat quietly for a while, sipping iced lemonade. Occasionally a firefly flitted by, lighting up the foliage that screened the veranda from Elm Street, which divided the Lambert house from Tod Elberton's.

Tod was a widower, living alone, acutely alcoholic. When he was not drinking, he either sat on his porch or whiled away the time inside his six-room house, once full of the laughter of his obese wife Sarah. Early in their marriage she knew she would never bear children and she had mitigated her sorrow in appetite. At thirty-five she died of diabetes.

For a while Mrs. Elberton fought her constant desire for chocolates but after a year of treatment, one night after Tod had gone to work in the Winterville Shoe Factory, she had purchased five pounds of chocolate drops and consumed them entirely. Next morning when Tod came from work he found her in a coma. She died within three days, and he had not known a day since when he did not seek escape through alcohol.

"Tod's not at home tonight," Mrs. Lambert said. "I saw him going toward Paw's Place."

"I've seen him entering the pool hall several times lately," Lizbeth said. "Sooner or later, every man and boy in this town finds his way to Paw's Place."

"Something should be done, but I—" Interrupted by the telephone, uncertain of its ring, she paused, listening with Lizbeth. It rang again and Lizbeth went to answer.

"I called to see when the tent meeting will be over," Jo said, when Lizbeth picked up the receiver.

Lizbeth's heart leaped, thinking their prayers had

been answered. "It ends next Saturday night," she said. "Usually they stay longer than four weeks, but the Reverend Redmond is called to South Carolina for the rest of the summer."

"That's good news. Kent said I couldn't give the housewarming until the meeting ended," she confided. "I told him about your visit and that's when he took that notion. He said he imagined a lot of other people from the Loganville churches were going to the tent. So if you're sure it ends next Saturday night, I'll run the announcement in *The Loganville Weekly* next week."

"I'm sure," Lizbeth said, disappointed once again. She had failed to win Charley Shedd to God. Must she always fail?

"Thanks and good-night," Jo said sweetly. "I expect to see you at my party."

Returning to the porch, Lizbeth relayed the telephone conversation. "That will give you some idea of what a soul winner I am," she said in despair.

"Sometimes we try to go above God," Mrs. Lambert said. "He has given you an assignment, but there are facets of every God-given task that He must do Himself."

Such as entering into a stubborn rebellious heart and changing it so that an aging man might forgive another a youthful error, she thought. Or taking a gay shallow little heart and reshaping it to His glory.

"Maybe you're right," Lizbeth said. "Anyway I'm glad she called. Somehow it makes me feel very close to her."

The Reverend Redmond telephoned on Saturday morning, with a special invitation to the tent that night.

"I do need to hear your sermon tonight," Lizbeth said. "I'm sorry I haven't been coming, but I think I explained to you about Mother. If I can arrange to have someone sit with her tonight, I'll come."

"I certainly hope so," he answered. "How is your friendship with your new neighbor?"

"I'm not sure I've accomplished anything," she confided. "I've visited her and I talked with Kent."

"That sounds all right," he said. "Then she isn't interested in the revival?"

"Apparently not. She telephoned Wednesday night to invite me to a housewarming party at her house next week."

"Seek every avenue to witness to this young woman," he said. "And keep me informed. If I can help you, just write me or call me." He gave her his address and telephone number in Marble Hill. "But then I think I'll see you tonight. In fact, I'll call you back in less than an hour and tell you what I've arranged."

"That's—fine," she answered, so surprised that she hardly knew what to say.

True to his promise, he called back in a half hour. Mr. Bill Godwin, a special worker at the tent, would drive by for her and Mrs. Lambert at seven o'clock that evening, he explained. "I've instructed Mr. Godwin to place your mother's chair near the altar. I've reserved a seat for you nearby. I look forward to seeing you both."

79

"Thanks, thanks so much," and as she replaced the receiver, she realized what this meant. She remembered Neal Redmond as he had impressed her at first sight, a gifted young man stamped with integrity and earnestness but a lonely person, almost pitiful in his zeal as he labored for God. And she thought, I wish it could be different. I wish I could return his affection, but I can never love anyone other than Cecil, however genuine he may be.

o   o   o

That evening when Lizbeth and Mrs. Lambert arrived at the tent, the Reverend Redmond greeted them warmly. Whatever reservations Lizbeth felt about him, her mother had her own ideas about this young evangelist. "You're the kind of son every mother dreams of having," she said. "I never had any sons myself, but I know mothers who did who would pay a big premium to swap for you."

He flashed Lizbeth a smile. "Maybe you could trade in your daughter," he suggested.

Mrs. Lambert's face beamed, Lizbeth noticed in embarrassment. "I hadn't thought of that," she said, studying Lizbeth for signs of interest in Reverend Redmond. "But I reckon I couldn't trade off Lizbeth. I don't know what I'd do without her."

He caressed her bone-warped shoulders and smiling again at Lizbeth, he returned back of the curtain. Not until the choir sang the initial song, "Bringing in the Sheaves," did he reappear and then it was as though he had forgotten that Lizbeth was present. His mind, heart, and soul seemed centered directly on the throne of God as he appealed, by the read-

80

ing of God's Word and by sermon, for lost sinners to come to the altar in complete surrender to the Savior of mankind.

After the benediction, after hundreds of people had hurried down the sawdust trail, Bill Godwin came to Lizbeth and asked if they were ready to go home. He told her the Reverend Redmond had been called to Johnston and that he was on his way now.

Lizbeth felt a pang of disappointment. She had wanted to discuss a point he had made about winning a person obviously in love with this world, to the Lord. He seemed like a rock in a storm, so secure and undisturbed by life's realities.

"I hope he can help that fellow," Bill said, when he stopped at the Lambert mailbox.

"What fellow?" she asked.

"A man staying tonight in the Johnston Hotel, traveling through," he answered. "Had a heart attack and sent for Reverend Redmond."

"Why him?" Lizbeth asked. "Does he know him?"

"He listens to him on his car radio," he explained. "He's a traveling salesman. He knows he's going to die but maybe there's time left."

"I hope so," she answered, but she thought, Time. Her heart racing, she prayed that there would be time left for this traveler and for Mr. Shedd and Jo, who had not yet expressed any interest in God's evangel.

10

□ A FIVE-PIECE ORCHESTRA, imported from Winterville, arrived only moments after Jo came downstairs on the night of the housewarming. Seeing her dressed in her black knee-length gown and tiny-heeled satin slippers, the musicians whistled. At the sight of her, they forgot Kathi Grant, the petite blond dancing-singing talent, with whom they had flirted over a hundred miles of freeway.

"Fabulous!" the florid-faced trombonist exclaimed, and the others apparently agreed. "Incredible to find such beauty hidden off in the mountains like this," he remarked.

Accustomed to such compliments Jo smiled graciously, and followed Kent who directed the band to the drawing room. When Cole Wilson's father built the long high-raftered room, he intended using it to entertain hundreds of cousins, nieces, nephews, and neighbors who came to visit. No bandstand had been erected and no dances had been held in that house previous to this night. But a week ago Jo had provided an improvised stage at the north end of the dining room. She ordered the piano, a baby grand, purchased for her initial entertainment, placed on the platform and here the musicians, after one glance over the length of the floor, felt themselves at home.

Afterward Kent found Jo in the kitchen, studiously watching an alkalizer sizzle in a glass of water. "Nothing's wrong, darling," she said. "I always get nervous before a party. Being on parade isn't as easy for me as people think."

"I'm nervous about this party, too," he said. "Coming on the heels of the tent revival, a jazz party like this. What will people say?"

"Who cares?" she answered flippantly. "Besides, if they're all here, what can they say? We're all in it together. The plans are laid."

"I'm not sure they'll all be here." He studied her face, beautiful with animation. "You invited everyone?"

"I ran it in the paper three days straight," she answered. " 'Public is welcome. House already adequately furnished. Guests are asked to bring no gifts,' so the ad ran."

"I know about that," he said wryly. "I took enough ribbing about that line. But seriously, I'm thinking about the church people. What will they say?"

"I don't know. Lizbeth Lambert is coming," she

answered. "She promised when she came to see me the other day. It's surprising, but I'm rather fond of her. At first I thought her dull, but if you study her closely, she's attractive."

"I'll have to look more closely." And he felt relieved that she was coming.

○   ○   ○

A half hour later Lizbeth arrived at the Wilson house and Jo greeted her warmly. She came alone. Ina refused to go, jeering at the idea of anyone welcoming not only a pagan, but the wife of one who brazenly disregarded the feelings of others.

Lizbeth herself had accepted the invitation reluctantly. She went, thinking that there she would find insight into Jo's character, something to use as a guide in helping her.

Everybody knew now of Jo's opinions on religion. They knew because people thrived on the sensational and certainly Jo was a sensation. Loganville had its share of godless people but never one like Jo. There had once been an aged man who lived on the hill at the rear of the Lambert house, a man named Sim Neeley, who claimed that there was no God, no heaven, and no hell. People referred to him as "that old infidel." Crowley Sutton, who worked the rails, came later. Mr. Sutton would not allow a Bible brought into his house.

And there was Charley Shedd, whose happiness and salvation Lizbeth longed for and prayed for. Still others, hardly noticed, went their way in Loganville, arguing by word or precept that there was a heaven but no hell, and some confused all religious truth.

But none of these had stirred up such interest as had Jo. It actually appeared that Loganville's citizens admired Jo's obstinacy.

Lizbeth was astonished that the Wilson house had changed so drastically to such sparkling festivity. Surely no hostess had ever appeared lovelier, or more glamorous than Jo. Though Lizbeth felt welcome to this house, there was in Jo's manner a warning that she did not want any mention of religion on this occasion.

In the ballroom, flanked by the pressing clusters of people, Lizbeth felt less alone, but lonely. When she went out socially, she still felt the loss of Cecil. She could work without feeling the loneliness, but in the gaiety of a social gathering her heart yearned for him.

The lively chatter in the gay rooms was stilled as the orchestra played several numbers and Kathi soloed two songs. When the last guests had passed down the receiving line, Jo and Kent, arm-in-arm, appeared at the door and announced dinner, served buffet-style, in the dining room.

Going from room to room, crossing hallways and corridors, Lizbeth was keenly aware of the magnificence of the old house, now laid with wall-to-wall carpeting, and illumined brilliantly with chandeliers. Buffet, smorgasbord, by whatever name it was called, it was abundant dining. There was wine in fine glasses. The silver, the china, the food—all reflected the abundance and good taste of the Wilson tradition.

As she mechanically chatted over food, some peculiar quirk of the mind momentarily transformed Lizbeth to her high school years. She recalled an English assignment when Miss Alberts had required each senior to present a paper describing his most recent social function. Except for Brenda Malone, who spent each Christmas with her aunt in Charleston, her classmates wrote sparingly of a basketball tournament in the Loganville High School Gymnasium.

Telling of a wholesome congregation of young people from various high schools in three adjoining counties, these were simple little narratives. They wrote sparingly because their area of vision was limited to simple small-town diversions. Like everything else, Loganville had changed since then. Glancing over the long room where people were variously occupied —talking animatedly, sipping cocktails, smoking cigarettes, laughing, joking—she was appalled that customs could change so rapidly.

The dancing that followed continued for much of the evening. Intermittently, Kathi performed several numbers, dancing as she sang gay frivolous songs.

Some time later, fearing that the enthusiasm waned, Jo went anxiously to Kent and whispered to him. She then mounted the improvised rostrum, motioned the professional dancer aside, and after a quiet consultation with the orchestra's leader, sang and danced a jazz song.

Jo had an untrained but faultless voice and her body kept the rhythm of the song's variations perfectly. At the end of the first number, she acknowledged the applause and again performed, mimicking Kathi's entire act in such an astonishing manner that Hank, the band conductor, asked Kent if she had once been a stage actress.

Kent thought, She is an actress. I absolutely cannot tell whether she is happy in Loganville or not.

When she finally left the stage, Kent met her with a complimentary glass of red wine.

Apparently Lizbeth was the first guest to leave. When she tried to locate Jo to thank her for the evening's entertainment, she found her surrounded by people, some of them loyal church members, who beamed their admiration and their envy. Among the group stood Miss Julia Lodge and her inseparable friend, Mrs. Drusilla Crew, widowed since World War II. Public school teachers, Sunday school teachers, and leaders of Loganville's youth groups, they complimented Jo for the "lovely party" and for her "unusual dancing and singing talent." Jo had won them all, the level-headed and the weak-minded. Intoxicated by her heady brand of pleasure, it seemed that all the people had fallen into a common web.

And the men. Each prided himself that he was a man and that times had changed. The fact that Jo was Kent's wife did not necessarily forbid their pleasure in her.

Lizbeth exited through the lower hall which led onto the patio. She wound her way through a narrow foliage-lined walkway from which she presently reached the fruit orchard, planted twenty years before Kent was born. Those two pioneers of the faith, Cole and Sadie Wilson, would have never conformed to the changing tide. Where were the wise? she wondered. Were there none left with faith and integrity to keep the dark paths lighted for mankind?

Lizbeth found Martha Lambert awake, awaiting her
return. She sat a while on her bedside, discussing
Jo's party. "Times have changed until it's like a
new world and new people," Lizbeth said. "Some
of my classmates are like strangers. Sue and Dale
Ingram, for instance. All through school they were
sweethearts, but Dale spent more time tonight flatter-
ing Jo than he spent with Sue."

"Poor little Sue!" Mrs. Lambert cried. "She must
have felt crushed."

Lizbeth vicariously shared Sue's dilemma. Serving
others, she had learned to shoulder problems that
did not directly touch her own life. "Most of the
modern women fight back with the same ammuni-
tion, adding fire to fire," she answered. "Sue turned
her attentions to Wiley Cofer. Wiley thinks he's a
gift to all women; so it was an easy quest."

"Lizbeth!" Mrs. Lambert exclaimed, astonished at
the unusual words that had entered into her conversation. "Working at that bus station is robbing
you of a finesse you once had. Everybody admired
you for it."

"Not many fighting soldiers are concerned with finesse," she said. "It isn't that I condone what is
wrong but it's necessary to know what is wrong. I
think it's what the Apostle Paul meant by being all
things to all people."

"I hope you know what you're doing." She sighed,
then continued, "I'm all for winning the lost, Jo of
all people, but I don't like to see you become a
worldly-spoken young woman. Lizbeth, you don't

realize how you've changed."

Lizbeth remained quiet a long time. She had changed, so that she might change others, but to her knowledge she had changed no one. And yet she had no accounting of having won a single soul to the kingdom of God. "It is disillusioning," she said. "Nowadays there's so much clamor, making a living and living it up, it's hard to hear the voice of God. Maybe I'm getting off the rails, after all. Sometimes I wonder if anything can be done. All the people seem to have lost their sanity."

The thought reminded her of Dr. Gilbert Findley, his hair silvery as platinum, who came once a week from Winterville to attend her father in his last illness. Not once did he leave without some new knowledge of the Lord's saving power, inspired by her patient father, but a year later the doctor had died, only minutes after his wife begged him to tell his anxious family whether he was prepared for death. He shook his head, beautiful with the vast wisdom residing in his brilliant brain.

"I can't believe," he said. "I could never understand that part. I tried, but God forgive me, there was too little evidence."

Too little evidence, she mused, recalling Jo's housewarming party. She had gone tonight, thinking it would tighten the link between them, so that she might find a way to understand her, but from the moment she entered the ballroom until now she had wondered and fretted.

               °   °   °

The following day she went to the bus station,

burdened with the memory of a party that would be remembered in a hundred different ways. At mid-morning Ina came to work, bringing a copy of the *Kensington County Daily*. In the woman's section, heading a long feature article on Jo's party, with Jo and Kathi respectively performing their separate song-and-dance acts, a picture of the orchestra pointed up the gaiety of the preceding night's event.

"A list of the guests is on page eight," Ina said. "Your name is on the list. So it's like I said, Logan-ville will have her blue bloods yet, but I hadn't thought you'd be one of them. 'Little Bus Station Princess.' Huh?"

Lizbeth laughed in spite of her dejection. How could she explain how she felt about having been one of the guests? Ina would not understand why she went; she questioned it herself. What was the right thing to do in winning a carefree unbeliever?

The Reverend Redmond would know. Tonight when her work was done she would write him a brief note, asking his advice. He could not heal her heart, nor could he convince her that she could bury her memories of Cecil. Until then she could not marry anyone and for this reason she must be tactful with the evangelist, keeping at a distance, while he led her to a closer altar in God's service than she had ever known.

11

☐ DURING THE WEEKS that followed Lizbeth learned that Jo had many fine qualities. She was a determined person and she kept her word. Once won to God's service she would be a great asset, and yet Lizbeth wondered if this would ever become a reality.

From all outward appearances, Jo did not stand more in the need of God than the average Christian. She accompanied Kent to church on Sunday mornings. Dressed fashionably and fastidiously, practicing impeccable manners wherever she went and in whatever company, she set the pace. The people admired her openly, forgetting her pagan beliefs. Actually they no longer believed that she was without God. Did not church attendance indicate that she trusted Him?

Who dared, except the self-righteous, to judge her? So as time went on, Loganville's citizens forgot that there was anything different or strange about Kent's wife.

The parties at the Wilson house continued. Frequently Kent and Jo were invited to similar functions at Loganville homes, but they went more often to Johnston, a small college town, to the theater or to cocktail and bridge parties. There gradually developed a lively interchange of invitations from house to house, among the most prominent families, in the two neighboring towns. This social activity satisfied a hunger in the lives of many people, some young, some of dubious age.

Lizbeth was undaunted. She could not shake the finality of the command: "Win Jo." Conscious now of wasted time, she was deeply grateful when Neal Redmond replied at once to her letter, giving counsel regarding her concern for Jo. He asked that she keep him informed of any progress she made in that direction. Regrettably, there had been none, and she did not answer immediately.

A month later, when the itinerant cotton pickers stopped daily for a quick lunch, he sent a copy of his book, *Are You Shutting God Out?* He had mentioned the book during his sermon the final night of the revival. She had intended to ask for a copy, but he left unexpectedly, and now she felt she could use it in one of her frequent visits to the Wilson house.

She answered his letter promptly to thank him for the book and for his thoughtfulness. As a closing paragraph she wrote:

Mother asked me to remember her to you. She was inspired and helped by your sermon and we both appreciated your making it possible for us to attend the tent services. I intend to present the book to Mrs. Wilson my next visit to her home. No apparent progress to report. Kent is as reserved as ever. Nobody knows what is shut up in his mind, nor how he feels about Jo's relationship to God. From all appearances, God is shut out of that house which was built on an unusually sturdy faith in God. Yet I have hope.

Sincerely in Christ,
Lizbeth Lambert

It was a business letter, deliberately kept in a detached vein. She knew—and he knew—that between them that day at the Baxley house an understanding had taken place in their minds, but not in Lizbeth's heart. She understood that he had been attracted to her but she did not know why. Except for Cecil, no man had ever shown more than casual interest. Although she now needed the evangelist's support, she hoped to make it clear that she no longer claimed the boundaries of her own heart. After posting the letter to Neal, she walked toward the Wilson house.

Jo welcomed Lizbeth with kind enthusiasm. Indeed, no one in Loganville had seen her ruffled or distressed about anything. Nor was she given to argument. As on previous occasions, sensing the full purpose of Lizbeth's overtures, she smiled and offered her a seat in the den where she and Kent had been reading *The Winterville Times.*

"Thanks but it's getting late," Lizbeth said, after greeting Kent cordially. "I brought you a book Reverend Redmond wrote himself. When you've read it, Jo, I want you to tell me what you think of it."

"So you can tell him?" She laughed, her teeth dazzlingly white filling her mouth copiously. "You know I always tell the truth," she challenged Lizbeth. "Would you relay that also to your Reverend Redmond?"

"We'll wait and see." Lizbeth smiled, glancing surreptitiously at Kent, who looked up from his reading, alert, interested.

"How's your protégée getting on with her Bible lessons?" he asked, lifting an eyebrow, averting his eyes so that none knew what he thought or wished to hear.

"Again we'll wait and see," Lizbeth answered. "I believe her report on Reverend Redmond's book will partly answer your question."

Jo appeared oblivious to the discussion of herself. Her mind had reverted to other channels, where she felt entirely in command. "I believe Lizbeth is quite fond of Reverend Redmond," she said. "A little bird told me he wanted to make her his wife—his second wife."

"Jo, maybe Lizbeth doesn't like your teasing," Kent cautioned.

"That's all right," Lizbeth said. "I know Reverend Redmond's a widower. But about the little bird—"

"The little bird is Mrs. Baxley," Jo admitted at once. Kent resumed his reading, a relaxed smile enhancing the lines of his lean profile. "Mrs. Baxley and Jo are confidential spies, I think," he said. "Sally brings Jo all the news and Jo has fun embroidering it."

"Kent!" It was Jo who scolded now. "You know one thing I don't do is gossip."

Lizbeth left soon, thinking of them as any normal couple except that God was not an integral part of their home. What Kent felt and believed was hidden so well that he appeared equally as callous as his wife.

Returning home, intending to visit the Shedds, Lizbeth walked fast, noting the rain streamers in the lowering sky over the pineland bordering the Wilson and Shedd farms. Rain, sunshine, sleet, snow—it was all the same to her tonight, her heart was so heavy and despondent.

o   o   o

Charley was not at home but Vi was overjoyed to see Lizbeth when she knocked at the kitchen door. Pouring a cup of coffee for Lizbeth, Vi joined her at the table. Her fingers drummed gently the yellow-flowered oil tablecloth.

"I went to his grave this morning," Vi said after a while.

Lizbeth set her cup down with a little clatter. "Had the chrysanthemums wilted? I carried them yesterday."

"They looked fresh enough," she answered. "I changed the water. Don't tell Charley but I prayed. Just a little prayer."

"Why not tell him?" Lizbeth asked. "It might

help him to change. You want him to love the Lord and trust Him just as we do, don't you?"

"I want it but I'm afraid it would only make him more determined in his unbelieving." She shook her head despairingly and then smiled, the blank smile of a dull mind. "I prayed for you, too. I prayed you would never stop loving Cecil." She started crying thin, pitiful wails. "I want you to have everything that belonged to Cecil."

Lizbeth sat quietly, waiting for rationality to return, as it would, after an interval. She was stricken for the first time with the abnormality of this household. A house without hope literally, guarding the memory of a loved one as a pagan worshiper of the dead. If Cecil had died in the Lord, then he was with the Lord, and his grave was empty as the corn husks.

"I've got something to give you," Vi said. Drying her eyes with her apron, she went into the room adjoining the kitchen. This was Cecil's room, kept as it was the day of his death, his tennis shoes and socks on the bare floor, the same printed bedspread he had used, his books on the table where he had left them prior to leaving the house to join Kent Wilson.

Vi returned shortly with a snapshot she had found that day while going through Cecil's chest of drawers. "Here's a picture of you. You keep it."

Lizbeth took the snapshot. Gay, laughing nineteen-year-old high school seniors, dressed in snug winter clothing, leaving the Shedd house hand-in-hand, they presented a picture of youthful happiness. This Charley Shedd had captured with the camera he and Vi had given Cecil the previous Christmas.

"We were just starting out on New Year's Eve to join the other seniors for a winter hayride over the countryside. Mr. Shedd drove his wagon and Herman Powers drove a team Mr. Cole Wilson sent to the town square. There were six wagons," Lizbeth reminisced quietly.

Vi's face clouded darkly. "I can't control my anger for Kent Wilson, not when I get to studying about it."

"That's how I felt," Lizbeth said. "I felt that way till I forgave Kent. Did Mr. Shedd tell you?"

"No, he didn't tell me," she answered tearfully. Her shoulders heaved and the sobs emerged in struggling, spasmodic jerks.

"You mustn't cry," Lizbeth said, drawing Vi close to her. "I still love you and Mr. Shedd and Cecil. But I love the Lord more than I love anyone. I have to keep His command."

Vi did not answer. After a while Lizbeth left, needing to get home before darkness fell. Soon Charley would return from the town, probably directly from the pool hall, and he would do for Vi all that could be done. But neither his presence nor his absence mattered to Vi during such outbursts. The one thing that would have helped her he had destroyed—her faith in God. It was truly a pitiable household.

12

☐ IN THE FALL when the cotton picking was done and the burs nakedly brown drooped under the constant rains that came with November's end, Lizbeth made another visit to the Wilson house. Jo, wearing a yellow silk kimono and matching quilted slippers, invited Lizbeth into the fire room, once used for all purposes when Cole and Sadie Wilson kept the house. Here they had made hamper baskets for harvesting; they had quilted, sewed, and read the Bible daily in this room.

Now a log fire glowed in the wide cavernous fire-place. Mrs. Mackey brought tea and buttered cube toast. A woman of enduring silence, she departed quickly and silently. From the first she had considered Jo a strange woman, an unfitting wife for Kent, and she had not changed her mind one iota.

"Lizbeth, I have the most marvelous thing to tell you," Jo said, her eyes showing excited pleasure. The two women conversed easily now, as though they were lifelong friends. "I'm going to have a baby. Imagine!"

"Why, Jo, how wonderful! I'm glad for you and Kent."

"I'll have a way now to use the pretty white Bible you gave me," Jo said. "Of course, the date of birth will go inside and I'll keep it in the nursery."

"What of the other religious pictures and the Bibles that you stowed away?" Lizbeth asked. "Will you bring any of them to the nursery? You know how a child treasures what belonged to his grandparents."

"Those antiques?" Jo grimaced. "They're only dust catchers. If you touch the paper on Granny Wilson's big old Bible, the leaves crumble like dried sage."

"But I'd keep them for Granny Wilson and for Miss Sadie," Lizbeth coaxed. "Those religious wall hangings and those Bibles meant everything to Kent's folks. If ever anybody loved and trusted God, it was Granny Wilson."

"Yes, there's evidence of that." She smiled, a starched lingering smile, her eyes at a standstill. "Imagine Kent marrying me. It just shows what love can do to a man. Anyway, I wanted you to be the first to know about our baby. We hope it's a boy. I want him named—guess?"

"Kent, Jr., I imagine."

"No, after Kent's father, Cole. It's an old family name. The first Cole Wilson was an evangelist."

She smiled, feeling that she had pleased Lizbeth. "He preached on the London streets quite frequently. That was before the family migrated to America. I imagine if he lived now, he'd be one of your tent revivalists."

"You are surprising," Lizbeth said, smiling thoughtfully, recognizing that this was only a peculiar whim, that Jo still had not trusted her heart to the Lord Jesus. "I thought every woman wanted her first son named for her husband."

"This woman is different," Jo said.

Lizbeth did not argue the point. Jo was indeed a pattern set apart. If only she believed! Then she might influence others for God as effectively as she did for the world.

"I'm fearful though," Jo said. "In this remote place and such a tiny outdated hospital, I'll probably die in childbirth. I do feel as though something abnormal will happen. It will be either me or the baby."

"Jo, you mustn't talk like that," Lizbeth said. "I'll pray for you and the baby."

"Lizbeth, I would be glad if you would." Though Jo did not believe for an instant that God was, or had ever been, somehow she felt that Lizbeth was stronger because she believed in God.

"But I must pray according to God's will," Lizbeth reminded her. "God has promised to supply all our desires if we trust Him and believe that He is able. But one must do that."

"He answers prayer, you told me that," Jo quickly reminded her.

"Yes, but often God doesn't answer prayer in the

way we expect," she explained patiently. "If He did, I'd be married now. I'd be Mrs. Cecil Shedd. If there hadn't been that terrible accident."

"I'm sorry I said that," Jo cried. "Do forgive me. Was it an automobile accident? Tell me about it."

Then Kent had never mentioned Cecil's death to her and assuredly not his part in it. "He died the night before we would have graduated from high school together," she said. "The day after graduation we planned to be married. Instead, we had Cecil's funeral. Mrs. Shedd offered all the lilacs on her tree to decorate the stage for graduation. Cecil's classmates took them down where they hung on the stage, and dropped them before the casket as they carried it to the cemetery."

Jo sat strangely still. "And you haven't forgotten him?"

"No, nor the way he died. I try to forget that part but I can't."

"Tell me how it happened, Lizbeth."

"How or why? Which do you want to know?"

"Both."

Lizbeth waited a while before she told her briefly but unsparingly of the fatal night. "Why Cecil died was partly his own fault," she said. "He knew it was wrong to speed on the highways and to endanger his life and the lives of other people. He liked fast cars, but when he got his driver's license, Mr. Shedd had exacted a promise that he wouldn't break the speed laws. If somebody older and supposedly a Christian hadn't influenced him, I believe he would have obeyed his father."

101

"Who influenced him?"

"Someone he admired very much," she answered. "All the young people copied that young man. But before I tell you his name, I must tell you I've forgiven him. It was Kent, your husband."

"Oh," Jo said, startled. "Oh."

"Please don't worry about it," Lizbeth said. "I've forgiven Kent now."

"And that wouldn't be easy, I'm sure. You lost everything. And if Kent was responsible—well, how could you forgive him?"

"Let's get it straight." Lizbeth reached over and touched her hand, begging full attention. "Kent influenced him, I'm sure of that. Cecil admired Kent, but it was Cecil's responsibility to choose what he knew was right. He knew auto racing was wrong. But I do think Kent influenced him. As I've said, I forgave Kent."

"That's just like you," Jo said wonderingly.

"I could do it only because of God's forgiveness," she replied. "He is ready to forgive anyone who comes to Him in repentance."

"Repentance," Jo mused. Then she shook her head. "Repentance of the past, maybe, if you believed at all. But promising to give up all the freedom, all the fun! Uh-uh. Too much to ask."

"No, Jo, not all the freedom and fun—you find in exchange a better freedom. Wanting to cling to worldly things dates back to the fall in the Garden of Eden."

"The Garden of Eden? Oh, Lizbeth, do you really believe that! Let me tell you about Mr. Gordon.

He was my boss before I married. He took me to the convention with him and there I met Kent, you know. He had a master's degree and he said in the college where he graduated they taught full length classes, teaching that it was all a myth. They persuaded the students, or a big part of them, to put it all down as myth and to simply sort out what they could believe if they persisted in believing any of it. Can't you see? It could never have really happened."

"What part of it could not have happened?" Lizbeth asked quietly.

"Oh." She spread her hands impatiently, the diamonds on her slender fingers sparkling. "Any part of it, I imagine, is a figment of the writers' extravagant imagination. Say, for instance, Peter walking on the ocean. Or Jesus."

Lizbeth drew on her gloves and got up to go. "I'd better get ahead of the storm,'" she said. "I'm sorry not to continue this conversation but I need to get back to the station ahead of the rain. Needless to argue over the Scripture, or I think not. Nowadays people are seeing more miracles than the children of Israel saw in their lifetime. When men travel in outer space, talking back to men on earth, and snap pictures of a man walking on the air, I wonder why it's hard to believe God has power to do anything He wills."

"But there was the rope to draw the astronaut back into the airship," Jo said.

There is always a rope when one trusts in God, Lizbeth thought.

She started to tell Jo that God never lets anyone who entrusts his life to His care get beyond the rope's tether, but Jo was not ready for that yet. Perhaps she would never be ready. If she did not win her, how would God judge Lizbeth, His servant? She did not know and for both reasons, she returned to the Greymount Bus Station in despair, needing to talk with Ina—or someone.

13

☐ INA WAS IN ONE of her darkly despondent moods, Lizbeth discerned as soon as she entered the station. "I feel so old," she confided. "When Herman and I courted, we didn't go anywhere much, maybe to the concert on the Square and to church. Sometimes we went for rides in the country. But the young people now think nothing of going to Winterville for a Saturday night movie." She paused and sighed. "You know Marie, who moved next door to me? Her daughters went last Wednesday night with their dates to Dave's Barn Dance in Winterville. They have a floor show there every night, kind of risqué, I gathered." She looked off into space and sighed.

"You don't mean you envy them?" Lizbeth asked.

"Well, maybe I do. We had such a short time together and if we'd had more fun, I could relive it when I'm alone."

Jo has done this thing to the people, Lizbeth thought. Before she came to Loganville, Ina grieved continually for Herman's soul.

Herman Powers had never made a public confession of faith and he had died in a pine field, his gun in his hand. All evidence pointed to suicide, but neither Ina nor any who knew him could arrive at a credible reason why he might have wished to end his life.

In the past Ina's grief and fear had been somewhat offset by the callousing effects of non-belief which she observed and welcomed in others. No God, then no heaven and hell; no hell, nothing to fear for the dead who might have died unsaved. So the current theory ran the gamut of one mind after another. But now there was a growing demand for pleasure, an antidote against remembering the past or thinking of the future.

Lizbeth believed Jo was, directly or indirectly, one of the most effective leaders of this new movement so far as Loganville was concerned.

"God is a mystery," Ina's voice held a little defiance. "I wish I knew Him better. Maybe then I could imagine how it is with Herman. At times he talked about God and how he should repent and live better. But can any past love for God spare him judgment?" Lizbeth might know, or she might find a verse in her Bible that would partially answer her question. Maybe sometime she could pray herself.

"Herman and I loved each other at first sight," Ina continued reflectively. But she could not tell Lizbeth just how it had been with her and Herman.

Ten years ago—the years had passed so astonishingly fast—Herman came with his father's threshing crew from Whitlock County, directly south of Loganville, to work in her uncle's wheat fields. He wore blue jeans and a hickory shirt, cuffs rolled above the wrists, and when he lifted his broad-brimmed hat, turned up rakishly on either side, he exposed a mop of thick straight black hair.

It was her task, as the adopted orphaned niece, to help with the farm chores. She carried water from the shady spring to the threshing crew, and as soon as Herman lifted the dipper their eyes met, his dark brown, hers the pale blue of his clean, frayed shirt. That was all the assurance they needed. Nor had they questioned their love, or asked the meaning of it. They knew; but Herman had spoken it when he glanced at his shirt and said teasingly, "Your eyes just match my shirt; so I guess we belong together."

"The past is all I have," she said pensively. "You just don't know how it was with us, Lizbeth."

Lizbeth did not know how it was to be married to the man one loved. Her life would have been completely different if Cecil had lived, if he had been wary of Kent.

"Why don't you remember how it was when your children were babies and Herman came home with candy or some treat from the store?" Lizbeth asked. "He loved you and the children. He was a good

neighbor, a good friend. And you have Felton and
Nellie and Scooter. Scooter is the sweetest two-year-
old I've ever seen. Why not remember that? Whatever you do, don't lose your faith in God. He's a
God of mercy and love, remember that."

"He had mercy on the thief on the cross," Ina
said thoughtfully. "That comforts me. But Herman
was a good person. It doesn't seem right to me that
a good person should lose his soul. I get to thinking,
maybe Herman was in trouble, maybe he owed a
gambling debt and saw no other way out. Lizbeth,
I can't get this off my mind."

"I'm sure it's hard, Ina. But don't forget that God
is love above everything else and in ways we can't
know. Don't lose your faith. Your children would
sense it and it would spoil their lives."

"Almost all the people are afraid of something,"
Ina said. "It's next to impossible to live a Christian
life nowadays. Everybody has so much to be afraid
of. They worry about debts of all kinds. The thought
of a stay in the hospital would drive a saint crazy.
Some people fear hospital bills more than death itself. We've come to dreadful times, I tell you. Some
people think God is dead or He would manage His
world better."

Her speech was actually a pathetic inquiry, a yearning for hope, and recognizing this, Lizbeth said, "God
is love. Love and cruelty are as far apart as the poles.
In all of life's changes, God's love is steadfast."

"You're just wiser than the rest of us," Ina said.
"We can't all be like you."

"I wouldn't want that," she answered. "What I'd

like to see is everybody trying to be as much like the Lord Jesus as possible."

Afterward Lizbeth remained silent and did not speak again until she went home. Occasionally she needed to keep quiet and ponder whether she walked the narrow path that a Christian in favor with God must walk. Tonight as she walked toward the Lambert house, she felt exceedingly dissatisfied with Loganville, with Kent and Jo and particularly with herself.

°   °   °

"Jo wants me to pray for her and the baby," Lizbeth confided to her mother later, as she washed and put away the supper dishes. "And I will. Whatever Kent may do, no matter what he has done, I can't help loving Jo."

Mrs. Lambert sighed. "Everyone sees something unusual about Jo," she said. "Some are almost persuaded to enter into a gay life of sin themselves rather than offend her."

Lizbeth nodded her head. "It's true," she agreed. "So true it's pathetic."

"What is it about Jo that makes people feel so about her?" Mrs. Lambert asked, her brow drawn into puzzled deep-set lines.

Lizbeth knew but she had too much compassion for Jo, who trusted her, to put it into words. What the people, and Lizbeth, found in Jo that drew them to her, both in admiration and in envy, was that careless abandon, that this-world-only gaiety. Indeed Jo had worked such wiles over Lizbeth herself that sometimes she forgot it was her purpose to show her the way to salvation, and not to entertain her.

"I believe Jo's charm is deeply rooted in something genuine none of us have yet seen in her," Lizbeth answered. "All but God have a blind spot when they look into the life of another. Maybe there is something about Jo we haven't detected."

٥   ٥   ٥

The following Sunday at sundown the town lay quiet under a red glow. The encircling wooded hills were touched with color and the stillness was broken only with church bells pealing. Lizbeth stood under the awning at the bus station, waiting for Neal to come by for her.

He had taken a three-day vacation from the pulpit and had telephoned to ask if he might see her. She invited him to go with her to First Church, remembering that he had long wanted to hear the Reverend William Corley preach. He had met him at a theological conference in the green lakes region of Wisconsin, but he had never heard him address a congregation.

"Well, hello; did I keep you waiting long?"

She turned, smiling, surprised. So engrossed in her thoughts she had been unaware of Neal's presence until he spoke. "Only a few minutes," she answered.

He laughed, noting that her practicality never wavered. Even in romance—he hoped she would sometime feel as he did—she spoke the unvarnished truth. "I parked my car at the back of the station," he said. "I intended to surprise you."

"And you did surprise me. But I am so glad you're here. I need your reassurance."

"But why, my dear?"

110

"Did you hear the bells?" she asked. "They seem sad this evening. I can't help feeling a bit forlorn myself."

At the car they stood a while, looking toward the Wilson farm. Since his father's death, Kent had enlarged the estate until his foothold on the earth was a small kingdom. Lizbeth, looking up toward the sky, wondered whether Kent had thought to lay away any holding—his heart, his soul—where neither moth nor rust would corrupt. "I can't help worrying about Kent," she said.

"Why not leave some things to God?" he asked as he started the motor and drove onto Loganville Road. "Maybe if we but knew, some we think are lost have only drifted a long way from God and will ultimately find their way back. The prodigal son returned of his own volition. You know, I can't help feeling that it is wrong to take too much into our own hands."

"But since Jo doesn't change, I hardly think Kent will make any change. I don't know what will happen to them. Their love for each other is deep but their home lacks something. God is simply not there."

He groaned. " 'What fools we mortals be,' " he quoted, wondering if Shakespeare had any conception of how many curtains God constantly pulled back to reveal the secrets of man. Man who could be big, little, magnificent, ordinary, good, wicked, lovely, hateful, and hated. Man who could be almost an angel or almost a devil. And yet who could understand the real Kent's, the real Jo's.

Neal glanced quickly at Lizbeth, his face reflecting

111

his concern for what so deeply troubled her. Turning at Grape Avenue onto Terminal Road they passed Mrs. Duncan's house where Lizbeth told him about the unique prayer garden. "Nobody had told me that," he said, deeply interested. But for this rare moment, he might have gone on, unenriched by this unusual incident.

"I'm sorry, I just now thought to tell you," she said. "Mrs. Duncan literally grieved for lost people. She had what so many Christians don't have—a compassion for others. Neal, nothing seems right anymore. Nothing except God."

"Ah, you have it quite backwards," he corrected. "If God is right there with you, if you're right with God, then it would be impossible for everything to seem wrong."

She sighed. "I'm sure you're right but I've failed them. I promised a dying boy and I promised God what I'd do. And I've failed."

"I'm not sure it's always the promising, Lizbeth. It's more the believing in God's doing."

After he parked at the back of the church, under a great oak tree, he clasped her hand. Looking directly into her eyes, he smiled, a smile of love and concern. Helping her from the car, he said, "Lizbeth, you'll never find happiness as long as you harbor bitter thoughts of Kent and I know you do. You say you've forgiven him and I know you try. But obviously you have not forgiven him. Isn't it time, dear one, that you trusted Cecil to God's care? I believe that might help to heal your heart."

Lizbeth nodded her head, but she turned away and

gazed back toward the river crossing. Her eyes flooded with tears, as she asked God to forgive her for the absolute hatred she once felt for Kent. "Kent is Thy child, too," she prayed silently. "Return to Thy household the prodigal son, so that all Loganville may rejoice and know that Thou art Jehovah God. Amen."

She turned then and they went quietly into the church. The half-filled sanctuary testified to the fact that most of the people present had forgotten the very purpose of the church, the assembling of His redeemed, manifesting that He came to give life everlasting, not only to them but to the lost everywhere.

14

□ ABOUT JO there was much that neither Kent nor Lizbeth nor any of her social set had yet detected. A woman with a many-faceted character, she revealed only parts of herself. What she did always appeared right and charming, and all semblance of design was generally lost on the observer.

So it was when she arranged with Mrs. Sally Baxley to invite the Reverend Neal Redmond to spend the Christmas holidays at the Baxley house. He would be near Lizbeth and he could also renew acquaintances made during his initial August ter: revival.

Mrs. Baxley, avid for a budding romance, complied readily. And eager to cooperate with whatever circumstance would unite him with Lizbeth, the Reverend Redmond accepted the invitation.

He arrived on the first Monday of December early in the afternoon. That morning a haziness over Old Brass Bald forewarned that snow would fall before night. At noon tiny flakes sifted over the valley and as he drove past the Greymount Bus Station a sugary snow lay over the town. He had not expected to see Lizbeth while she was busy at the counters inside the station, but he felt a nearness to her knowing she was there. He anticipated calling her that evening when her workday ended.

As he approached the Baxley house, Neal Redmond watched the clouds, discerning a threatening storm of blizzard proportions. Antioch Church was expecting him for the Sunday morning service and he was scheduled to perform the wedding of Ralph Staples and Ruth Hawkins at three o'clock in the afternoon. He definitely needed to get back to South Carolina, but if detained in the mountains because of the snow, it would be the first time he had broken an appointment since he started his ministry seven years ago.

Sally Baxley also believed a snowstorm imminent and for this reason she arranged with Martha Lambert that Neal should have luncheon at her house. Within an hour, he accordingly headed his car back toward Loganville. The snow, whipped now by a hard-driven northeast wind, froze as it fell on his windshield. The wiper, thumping steadily, helped little now and he drove most of the way looking from the rolled window.

As planned, he stopped for Lizbeth at the station. She knew of their plan—Mrs. Lambert had eagerly informed her by telephone—but none of it had impressed her. But she could not conceive of Reverend Redmond driving on such an inclement day over the hazardous mountain roads.

"I'm glad to see you," he said, after her reluctant greeting. "I know it appears foolhardy but it seemed a good idea to me. And I'm happy to drive through a storm—to see you again."

Lizbeth took off her apron, thankful that Ina was serving the booth counters. She could not tolerate another matchmaker. "I hope you're in the mood to help make soup," she said. "I can't remember much else we have on hand. The pantry reeks of emptiness."

He smiled and bit at his under lip, a habit when wryly amused. "I like marketing," he said. "Maybe I can go to the grocery store for you while you work this afternoon."

Lizbeth did not wish to appear harshly practical but sometimes her days' unchanging routine became overwhelmingly burdensome. Although she considered her breadwinning duties as trivial and she had energy to operate her job and the household, her spiritual and emotional unrest exhausted her.

"I'm glad you came anyway," she said, as he drove up the hill toward the Lambert house. "I still say driving in this weather is crazy, but so much that happens these days is crazy."

"People worry so much about 'these days' as though people and even God had changed." He suddenly snapped his fingers. "That's it," he said. "Now I have it."

"What?" she asked, noting the intensity of his

116

eyes, the set line of his jaw. He had changed instantly from the eager suitor to the evangelist, appearing now as she had first seen him in the pulpit. "What changed you so suddenly?"

"I've found the line for next Sunday's sermon," he answered. "It ties in with a poem I cut from an evangelical magazine last week. I hoped then to build a sermon around it but until now, I didn't know how."

"Where will you preach?"

Stopping in the yard to survey the housetop whitened by the fast falling snow, he shrugged his shoulders. "If I'm not snowed in, I'll be back in Marble Hill, preaching at Antioch Church."

Mrs. Lambert was obviously delighted to see them come in, and she shrugged off Neal Redmond's suggestions that he might be "trouble" as he intimated when Lizbeth started preparing pineapple sandwiches. "Don't worry about the snow either," she scolded. "It has always snowed. People now are afraid of snow. Lots of things they ought to be afraid of they're not, I'll guarantee that."

Neal stopped stirring the mixture of canned tomatoes, leftover stewed beef, sliced onions, generous seasoning, and only he knew what else, and stared unbelievingly at her. After starting the coffee to perking, Lizbeth had delegated the soup-making to him, since he insisted that he was quite familiar with the process.

"Mrs. Lambert, you've voiced my sentiments," he said. "People have changed in their attitude toward just about everything—even God. They seem to expect God to change and come down to their level."

"You should preach on that subject sometime," Mrs. Lambert suggested.

Nodding toward Lizbeth, he smiled. "Just what I was telling your daughter on the way up here," he answered.

"You talked over your sermon for next Sunday," she said, as she studied Lizbeth, hopefully believing that they might have reached some agreements.

Lizbeth hardly knew which way to turn. She loved these two good people and she did not want to offend them. Yet they could not understand her deepest feelings for Cecil despite the years—or could they?

After a wonderfully warm and nourishing lunch, Lizbeth walked back to the station. Though Neal had insisted on driving her back to her job, she finally convinced him that he would be doing a good turn by staying with Mrs. Lambert in case she needed anything. She suggested, too, that it would be a good time to prepare his Sunday morning sermon.

The snow, heavier by the hour, glorified the woodlands and fields but intensified the already hazardous highway conditions. Neal, thus warned, drove back to the Baxley's at five o'clock, leaving word for Lizbeth with Mrs. Lambert that he had his sermon fully prepared and that he would see her again before he returned to Marble Hill.

o   o   o

Next morning Lizbeth waded through the snow, making her regular visit to the Wilson house. She invariably chose the ten-to-twelve period, since Kent did not come home for lunch until around one o'clock.

She went with an extra purpose today and before she had spent a half hour with Jo in the breakfast room, she had found an opportunity to mention the nursery. "I know it's simply beautiful," Lizbeth ventured.

"I have it completely ready," Jo said eagerly. "Want to see it?"

"Of course," she answered, following her across the kitchen, into the back porch, and into the lower hall, timing her quick energetic steps to Jo's slower walk. Jo had grown much heavier and her periodic clinical reports had been far from satisfactory.

When Jo opened the door, Lizbeth exclaimed, "How lovely!" She admired the ruffled blue organdy curtains, the dainty blue gingham on the walls, and the white satin padded bassinet. Jo had everything a mother could desire for her expected child and her happiness was evident as she proudly surveyed the nursery as though seeing it for the first time.

Lizbeth went to the diminutive wall table to pick up the white Bible she had given Jo. "I'm glad to see you're using the Bible," she remarked. "Neal asked about you yesterday. Next time I see him I'd like to tell him something you said about his book. You've read it?"

"I started to read it but something came up. I think I had to go somewhere with Kent and I've just never got around to it again."

"The part you read—how did you like that?"

"So, so," she answered dubiously. "I'm afraid I don't understand a thing about this salvation he talks about. This God my parents sought after and never quite found, why is He so evasive? I mean, so hard to get to know?"

"People have made Him appear that way," Lizbeth said. "Maybe they didn't intend it that way and it may be only an excuse not to know Him. To know God is so many things. It is to believe on Him, to love Him, to trust Him, and at the same time to fear His judgments. It takes a lifetime to understand Him, Jo, and more."

"I'll read it," Jo promised. "I think I like your evangelist, as a man, that is. Why don't you?"

"I do like him," Lizbeth said. "I admire him very much."

"Of course, but why don't you love him?" Jo said. "The husband-wife kind of love. Why don't you encourage him?"

Lizbeth could not reply. She departed a few minutes later, thinking, If only Christians would work together in ·God's kingdom work and not spend so much time on personalities and speculations and trivialities.

15

☐ AS IT TURNED OUT, the weather permitted very little travel or communication. Telephone lines froze and broke. Electric power failed; gas lines struggled to supply fuel for heat and cooking.

Thursday and Friday Neal could not leave the Baxley house. On Saturday he walked to town to send a wire to the Antioch Church secretary, stating that he would be unable to preach Sunday morning. Ruth Corley, chief operator at the telephone-telegraph office, dispatched the wire, making mental notes which she relayed to her father, the Reverend William Corley, pastor of Loganville's First Church. By evening he had contacted Neal and invited him to fill the pulpit of First Church the next day.

Surprised at the invitation, desiring himself to hear

121

the Reverend Corley, Neal wished he could inform Lizbeth of this news. But the Baxley telephone had not been repaired. That afternoon, prior to this arrangement, he had stopped by the station to talk with her and to see if her mother needed him. She had sent him back to the Baxley's, saying that Mrs. Lambert had everything she needed and that she herself could walk up that hill better than he could drive. He readily complied, avoiding Lizbeth's disapproval. She was a practical young woman—very practical—but he loved her.

Lizbeth was therefore unprepared for Neal's appearance in the First Church pulpit on Sunday morning. Wearing for this occasion a clerical collar and a black robe, he appeared more professional and distinguished than ever, yet there was no arrogance in his bearing. Lizbeth felt a certain pride of possession in him now. He did belong to her, after a fashion—they were partners in God's service.

She watched him studying the congregation until he found her. He flashed her a smile and returning the smile she thought, How wonderful it would be if we were right for each other!

When the preliminary service ended and the Reverend Redmond announced his subject, "Has God's Law Simmered Down to Fit Your Needs?" she wondered whether Kent Wilson was present.

If anybody needs to hear this sermon, it is Kent, she thought. She feared to judge, but Kent had admitted in one of their discussions during her visits at the Wilson house, that he didn't practice what his parents had taught him.

And yet it was a sermon for everyone. "The lines of demarcation must be observed by all soldiers if the battle is won," the evangelist said. "God's laws were not written for a few but for everybody. Nor can God's law be broken by a few choice people with no resultant punishment. God is no respecter of persons." He warned of the prevalent trend to "wish away" the austerity of Jehovah God. "A God of mercy and love cannot but be a God of austerity," he said. "You who love your children are merciful when they err, but you sternly forbid them to do what you know will destroy them."

He cautioned the silent listening people against thinking that "the times," the horror of wars and famine, violence within and without the nation, might be possible reasons why God would soften His judgment of sins. "God's law is immutable, changeless as the sea." He held up the Bible and challenged one and all to try changing one jot or tittle in the sacred Word of God.

After the benediction, Lizbeth waited in the vestibule. Neal found her there, after most of the congregation had greeted him at the door, among these being Kent who seemed dissatisfied with the unusually eloquent sermon. When Neal came to her, he too seemed uneasy.

"I have arranged with Bill Godwin to drive my car to Marble Hill when the roads become passable," he said. "I have to rush for the train. Bill has chains on his tires and he's promised to drive me to Johnston."

"Mother will be disappointed," she said, feeling

a secret pang of disappointment herself.

"Tell her I'll come again when the snow season is over. And, Lizbeth, you know I'll come." He offered his hand and left with the briefest of goodbyes.

16

☐ SNOW FELL AGAIN the first day of February, surprising the people of that region for its unusual depth. Since Neal Redmond's visit to Loganville in December, several snows of varying intensity had fallen, but the present surpassed anything the people had seen in several decades. A blizzard followed the snow, freezing fast tiny particles of added precipitation. Temperatures dropped while the winds rose. Livestock froze. Buses and trains were off schedule. Traffic on the highways was almost nil.

At midnight, at the height of the blizzard, Jo sent Kent for Dr. Bell, positive that her baby would be born before dawn, although two months prematurely. Kent had not anticipated unpredictable weather conditions. Born of daring disposition and into an

125

era that never doubted the invincibility of man's ingenuity, he believed there was nothing modern invention could not conquer. To top this incongruity, the telephone lines were down and he could not get a call through to Dr. Bell. His plans to send Jo by ambulance to the Winterville Hospital had terminated with the freezing sleet and snow.

He walked at snail's pace; sometimes he crawled until he descended the icy drive to the foot of the hill. Already numb with cold, he gained the public road and quickened his steps to arrive at the doctor's apartments by midnight. He found him, awake and drinking a cup of black coffee in his living room, trying to read a ponderous medical book. Aware that on such a night only a miracle could prevent a baby's urgent birth or an old lady falling and breaking a hip or an asthmatic patient's sudden attack, he was fully dressed, his overcoat and rubber overshoes by his chair. He readily admitted Kent who had previously engaged him, in case of emergency.

"I came about Jo," Kent said now, answering Dr. Bell's unspoken question. "Telephone's out of order. Couldn't get out in a car. Can't possibly get her to a hospital. Guess we'll have to walk, if you'll go."

The doctor poured a cup of coffee and Kent took it with stiff nervous fingers. "Drink it down while I get into my overshoes and topcoat," he ordered. "You left someone with her?"

"Mrs. Mackey's with her. The housekeeper."

"This baby's two months premature. People get excited when it snows. This isn't a false alarm, you think?"

Kent shrugged. His actual knowledge of a birth was absolutely negative.

Everything this night was beyond his calculation. A product of the mountains himself, he felt a foreboding in Mrs. Mackey's manner. He felt certain that the sword of Damocles hung over their heads. The judgment occurred to Kent in the bitterest way he could be punished and he believed he heard the declamation: "You shall not have everything."

A moment later, Dr. Bell said, "Let's go."

Kent set the empty cup on the side table and followed him outside. A white world glowed in subtle beauty as though thousands of lights canopied Loganville.

"I'm sorry you'll have to walk in this slippery snow," Kent said.

"You forget that I have my horse," Dr. Bell explained as he turned toward the stables at the rear of the house. "I'll get there ahead of you. Shall I go in?"

"Yes, please do. Jo's looking for you."

Dr. Bell hurried; he hardly knew how not to hurry. And he thought, All husbands are alike in this hour, if no two men are ever in any other moment exactly alike.

o   o   o

Jo's baby, a six-pound boy, was delivered that night two hours after Dr. Bell arrived at 2:30. Kent rejoiced, immediately forgetting his resolve to be done with the future fatherhood of children, especially since Jo appeared in fine spirits. Dr. Bell at first believed Jo had come through her ordeal satisfactorily but he

127

never for a moment believed the baby was as well as he should be. His cry was weak, his body shriveled, but he quietly pronounced him "a fine boy."

To Kent privately he recommended an immediate consultation with a Winterville pediatrician. Further examination and clinical studies might reveal what he suspected, a congenital malfunctioning heart.

"We'll have a half dozen," Jo told Kent later, when he sat by her bedside. "It's really nothing after it's over."

Kent's effort to appear enthusiastic fell flat. "I don't know about a half dozen. Getting it over seemed an eternity to me."

Eternity. Jo pondered his remark. Why did Kent talk to her about this eternity, this heaven and hell, which he assuredly believed in, and yet did not actively prescribe for others?

Though deeply ingrained with spiritual teaching, Kent was unaware that his words indicated dormant convictions. He had no idea how the uncertainty of believing nothing, of knowing nothing, tore Jo apart. Except when she was in good spirits, acting out the clever abandon she had discovered worked such wiles over everyone, her whole being was in turmoil.

The neighbors went to see Jo and the baby but they came away slowly and reluctantly. It was hard to imagine Jo in the mother-role, expecially the mother of a baby who had been born physically deficient. Kent was a perfect specimen of manhood and not many women exceeded Jo's beauty and charm. Those who went to the Wilson house returned, each with a different story to tell.

As soon as the ice melted sufficiently for her to walk up the hill, Lizbeth made her way toward the Wilson home. The snow had melted, giving way to a blustery dry wind shipping into the valley. At the Swanson house the odor of fried navy beans, cooking on the black range, drifted through the air as she paused a moment, fearful of the long black hound dog that came toward her.

"He'll not bite you," Mrs. Swanson called from the kitchen's shutter window. "He's more bark than bite."

"Fine, thanks," Lizbeth shouted above the wind.

"Going to see the baby?" Mrs. Swanson called again.

"Yes. I'm ashamed not to have been there before now."

"Well, no need be," Mrs. Swanson said, shaking her head. "It's going to die. That poor little thing can't live with a shriveled up heart."

Lizbeth started to answer but there seemed nothing to say. She marveled that the mother of six children did not understand that like any parents, Kent and Jo would cling to the last tenuous breath of life for their child.

∘   ∘   ∘

Jo sat in the kitchen, sipping a cup of black coffee, and she poured a cup for Lizbeth. No longer needing to entertain Lizbeth except as an affectionate friend, Jo remained in this room for their morning visit.

Through the window Lizbeth watched the pines battling the swift wind. When she had visited here in her youth, she had wondered why Cole Wilson

129

planted pines, such lonesome trees, in the yard outside the kitchen window. Now she knew that in their spirited way of life, the Wilsons had felt no loneliness. Grandparents, parents, aunts, uncles, cousins—all of them were staunch Christians. For them life was joyous and rich in purpose. God first, God if nothing else, God before all else—this was the greatness of the Wilsons.

Jo gave a brief and apparently painful résumé of the baby's condition. "He's no better," she said. "We plan to take him tomorrow to the Winterville Pediatric Clinic for further X-rays."

"Jo, I pray something can be done," Lizbeth said simply.

She sat darkly silent for a while, then brightening, said, "Thank you, my true friend. And, Lizbeth, this will surprise you. Last Sunday I had reason to thank your God for something."

Lizbeth sat forward hopefully. "Yes? Tell me."

"You know, I'm a job widow," she said. "Kent is bent on becoming Loganville's first millionaire. But on Sundays most businesses close; so he has to stay home with me. I don't believe your Neal's 'Demarcation' sermon did anything for him. He's too bent on being the top man on the totem pole."

"Maybe it helped more than you can see," Lizbeth suggested.

"I hardly think so," she said stubbornly. "I do think though that your God did a masterful thing when He set aside one day a week for rest. Or diversion or whatever anybody wants to do."

Lizbeth agreed. "It was only one of the masterful

things He did. Some people get the wrong idea about Sunday. It's for rest and worship but I hardly think He intended it for selfish pleasure. Yet how can you make people understand?"

Jo laughed but now her laughter was restrained. Motherhood and its inherent concern had marked her whole being. "Lizbeth, honey, you can't make the world over," she said. "Maybe it needs it. A lot is wrong, I see that, but I just accept it."

Lizbeth knew the Wilsons had not accepted prevailing conditions. They conscientiously expected great and good things of Kent. It had never entered their trusting minds that he would scorn the three hundred acre farm and the cool high-walled homestead with its seasoned treasures, warmed by decades of love and hope.

She finished the coffee and arose nervously. "Before I go would you mind letting me see Mrs. Wilson's Bible, the big one Kent's great-grandmother brought over from England when they came here to settle?"

Jo looked at her wonderingly. "Lizbeth, you can see anything in this house you want to see." And she led her to the small room where she had deposited all the Bibles and mottoes. The room was starkly vacant except for the religious relics lying in a heap in the middle of the floor.

Lizbeth leafed fleetingly through the Bible, topping a stack of old hymnals. The Bible looked like an unabridged dictionary, its edges frayed, the paper yellowed. Then she glanced sadly at the religious pictures, at the good books, recalling what they had told her about God in this house.

Later as they tiptoed into the nursery, watched around the clock by three trained nurses, she noticed the little white Bible she had given Jo and her heart revived with a spark of hope.

"Here he is," Jo whispered, bending over the bassinet. "Come see our Buddy Boy."

Lizbeth looked at the wrinkled little face, pinched with the struggle to continue his hard breathing. She prayed silently, asking the protection of a loving God on Jo's child, for this was not a child of Kent's. Though he tried valiantly to form him into his own image, commanding the nation's best doctors to make him whole, as he had been whole, Kent Wilson had not accepted this child.

"Do you think he'll ever make it?" Jo asked when they went into the hall.

"Jo, this is in God's hands."

"That's exactly what Dr. Springhaur told us," she sighed. "Kent sent me to Winterville for a checkup yesterday. I wish I hadn't gone. I'd rather not know."

"What had you rather not know?" Lizbeth asked, thinking she had further confidences to reveal about Buddy Boy.

"I'm barren," she answered frankly. "Dr. Varner told me so. I'll never conceive again."

"Jo, I'm truly sorry," Lizbeth said. "Sometimes doctors are mistaken—"

"Not this one," she interrupted. "He explained but we'll skip details. He's sure. I'm simply one of those one-child mothers. Kent is about out of his mind. There's no comfort anywhere. If he can't get any comfort from God, how can I expect to find any from you and your church?"

"Have you tried?" Lizbeth asked. "Have you asked God to help you? Have you read the little white Bible in the nursery?"

"No. But I pick it up every day and look at it and I wonder how so many people could be duped by such a very tiny book."

"Many people read it, searching for help for themselves or others." Lizbeth said. But she could not draw Jo further on the subject. Yet as she started back on her windy route to the Greymount station, she knew that Jo was thinking. At least, it was a beginning.

Lizbeth gave thanks for this bit of hope. So preoccupied was she that not until she reached the station did she remember that she had wanted to tell Jo about the latest letter she had received from Neal Redmond. It was filled with anticipation of another tent meeting in Loganville, beginning the first of August. And in between the lines, there had been a most apparent anticipation of seeing Lizbeth again. Remembering, Lizbeth blushed.

17

☐ MARCH HAD COME in like a lamb that year. The warm sun through the weeks had melted the snows and the earth was dry by the time the month ended. And then with a sudden and violent curtaining of the skies, winds rose, bringing cold rain lashing across Old Brass Bald. Even the cattle shivered in their stalls.

It did not dismay the Holy unto God people who came biannually to preach repentance and salvation to the lost, and fire and damnation to the Christians who had turned their backs on God. No announcement was made of their coming and the evangelist was not introduced by newspaper notice. But a big tent was set up at the corner of the broom sedge field across the road from Logans' Undertaking Establishment.

134

For three days and nights it rained relentlessly. Men who worked outdoors, getting ready for the April planting, grew impatient. Needing to work and yet anxious for any excitement that idleness offered, they wandered into town. In addition to the steady customers, Paw's Place was the final assemblage for most of Loganville's men, including Charley Shedd.

Now he stood by the gaming tables, watching grumpily. He was still vexed with Brother Meadows who, after a visit with Vi last night, had reproved him privately for his alleged lack of faith.

"Your wife's recovery depends on your faith in God," he had said. "You may say you don't believe in God but she does. She believes Cecil is with God and in good hands. She could adjust and live a normally happy life if you believed that, too. You understand?"

"Yes, but I don't have to agree with you just because you're a preacher." His reply was sharp. "Maybe there is a God but the way He manages the world doesn't make sense. None of it makes sense."

Now as Charley stood at the gambling stands, perpetually astonished at the varied methods employed by different men, he put aside his fury. His addiction for watching gambling scenes equaled that of any participant present. The tense metallic sounds, mingled with occasional bursts of obscenity, excited him. Not actively engaged in any of it, his pleasure came from observing men more evil than he felt himself to be.

Finally he sauntered over to a huddle of men leaning on a vacant stand. Here he spent an hour discussing the weather. Haney Hargrove, not ready to end the talk, commented, "I'll bet the Holy unto God people will all take pneumonia and die."

"What you bet?" Thad Walters challenged. "God looks after children and fools."

Charley laughed. "They may take pneumonia," he agreed. "But they'll be there when the door opens. They haven't missed a night yet and it's rained the last three nights."

"I'll bet they don't leave here till the Ocmaha River runs dry," Thad said. "They're stubborn as an ox with that old-time religion."

Charley laughed, too, enjoying the banter. It was a pity that Lizbeth could not see through people like the Holy unto God band and the other evangelists who came with their loud, dark prophecy, he thought, as he sauntered back to the pool tables. He watched a while longer and then walked toward the bus station to see how Lizbeth did.

     o   o   o

"They got back, did they?" he remarked, after an exchange of greetings. "They thought they'd come back and stir everybody up, did they?"

"Brother Meadows is a layman," she explained. "He's never been here before to preach and I wish you'd go to hear him. He is heir to an oil fortune in Texas, but he's giving his whole life to God's service. I think that's wonderful."

Charley shook his graying head doggedly. He stubbornly refused to tell her that the layman-evangelist had called at the Shedd house the night before and had rebuked Charley for his agnostic statements.

136

"Plenty of good churches for people to go to," he argued now, as he had argued last night with his uninvited guest. "I say if people want to believe any of it, why don't they go along to some nice church with other people? Not get all fretted up in a tent meeting. No good in it."

"If they love God—" She stopped, watching the dark countenance, hushed by his quick silence. "I'm fond of you, Mr. Shedd. You're Cecil's father and I shall always have a place for you and Mrs. Shedd in my heart. So I'd rather not disagree with you. It's just that people need God so much. However they seek Him, I think it's better than indifference or open rejection of God and the church."

"If they're looking for God, why do they go off on such tangents to do it?" he asked, accepting the coke Lizbeth handed him.

"If all the people in Loganville knew that somewhere there was a fountain of good health, probably every one here would search till they found it," she said. "But no two would likely follow the same route."

He shook his head again. "Lizbeth, if you were my daughter, I wouldn't let you go to these tent meetings. I don't believe in tent meetings." He finished his coke and with a final "Come see us," he hurried from the station.

Lizbeth watched him out of sight and turned slowly back to her work. He was a constant reminder of the unfulfilled promise she had made to Cecil and to God. Nor had she yet found any interest in salvation on Jo's part. As a soul winner Lizbeth felt she was a pronounced failure.

137

Yet waking or sleeping, or working at the bus station, Lizbeth sought ways to expedite her assigned task. On Wednesday, following her initial visit with Jo, as she helped Ina close the counter for the day, she wondered if she should invite her to have a part in the undertaking.

Part of the town was asleep. Some had settled down for an after-supper rest before retiring. Occasionally the squeal of a tire, the excited chatter of dating teenagers, or the cries of small children drifted into the station. Cicadas on the river banks had spread out over the valley, their notes shrilling from the plum thicket bordering Greymount's parking lot. She decided against confiding in Ina when a Greymount bus pulled into the parking lot.

Running late, the driver had curtailed the usual rest stop, but he came into the station to consult with her about schedules. She went outside the counter to greet him. He was new to the route and therefore someone to whom she had not witnessed. She wondered what she could say to him before he maneuvered that long two-tiered express bus over the winding mountain roads, headed for New York and all points north.

"Good morning," he called cheerfully and glancing at Ina, he added, "Fine morning, pretty girls. What more could anyone ask?"

"God's grace," Ina answered.

"What?" he asked, astonished. Recovering himself, he smiled appreciatively. "Sure, I have that, I think. At least, I believe in God and I try to do what's right. But you surprised me for a time there. I

138

didn't expect it in a bus station."

"Why not?" she asked. "It's the most important thing on earth and in heaven—God's grace."

He agreed wholeheartedly and left whistling, his spirits apparently revived. God's grace could yet be found, sometimes in the laughter of a happy child, frequently in a mother's soothing touch, and in many other ways, Lizbeth observed. Perhaps none of it compared with a stalwart man whistling because he had within his own heart the grace of God.

"I was so glad to hear you witness to the driver," Lizbeth said. "I'm sure you spend less time grieving for Herman."

"I'm sure, too," Ina said. "I've found peace. Last night at the tent I turned my whole life over to God. Brother Meadows preached that in his sermon. He said it was the only way to show God how much you trusted and loved Him. Somehow I feel now that He'll take care of Herman for me. What happened to me last night is a pure miracle."

"God's power in any life is a miracle," Lizbeth said.

Another soul returned to God, she thought happily. But she felt sad that, to her knowledge, she had brought no one yet to the throne of God.

18

THE WILSON BABY did not get better. By the time the lilacs bloomed on Vi's tree, when he should have been pulling up and reaching for things, the only notable change was lengthened bones and increasingly sallow skin. In his daily struggle to withstand the onslaught of medicines and inoculations, he twisted and fretted. Waking and sleeping, his little face reflected his effort to find ease.

Jo watched him in his crib, waiting for Dr. Bell to arrive. After a severe choking spell, Kent had gone for the doctor. "Strangled on air," Mrs. Mackey told Jo the first time he started gasping for breath, but later Dr. Bell advised her to call him immediately if she recognized similar symptoms.

Preparing for the doctor's visit, she dressed Buddy

140

Boy in a long white cotton gown. In one of his rare quiet moments, when the straight black-haired head rested easily against his satin pillow, she thought he looked like a doll. On the coast one Christmas when she was seven, her father brought her a doll, purchased in a South American port city. Watching him, immobile in his crib, she marveled that the baby and the doll could look so much alike.

The doll long ago had had no beauty and at first she had been angered with the gift. Flailing the limber straw body against the round-bellied coal heater, she had broken its right arm. Seeing it on the floor, rejected, broken, she had seized it and rocked it in her arms, singing soothing lullabies. Later during the holidays her father had bought a beautiful doll dressed immaculately in white from bonneted head to slippered feet. Though she had accepted the second doll gratefully, she knew that no doll could claim the love she now felt for the frail ugly port city doll, for whose broken body she took the blame.

Her child's body too was frail and broken. What she had done to cause this she did not know. But from the first she knew that something was wrong. Until now she had kept her premonitions to herself, but when Kent came from the clinic, looking tired and dejected, she decided impulsively that the time had come to speak frankly.

"Dr. Bell will be on as soon as he finishes a clinic emergency," he told Jo, going anxiously to the crib to look at his son. "If he could just—" He stopped and did not finish the sentence.

She stared at his clenched fists. "You think you

141

can make him over into your image," she accused angrily. "Well, you can't. He's my poor little broken doll." She leaned over and kissed the small pinched face. "He's—"

"Don't you 'doll' my son," he snapped, grief overwhelming his reason. "It's no way to talk to a boy."

"He is like a doll," she persisted, forgetting her anger, understanding now that Kent could not help feeling bitter. His dreams for a son patterned after himself had collapsed, but still he hopefully tried to force the child's wholeness. "He's like the doll Daddy brought me from South America. There were millions of pretty dolls in all the places he went but he brought this doll." She smiled, her face reflecting nostalgia. "At first I felt about the doll as you do about Buddy Boy. But I grew to love it and that's the way I love our baby."

He started to reply, but Dr. Bell rapped at the door. Jo slipped from the nursery, too angry with Kent to watch her baby's examination. She went to the bedroom she shared with Kent and falling across the bed, she let come the great sobs that shook her weary body. Her past grief for her child had dried her tears. This new torrent was for something the broken doll symbolized—a nostalgia for her first broken home. Nothing in her life had ever been completely whole, she realized.

A blessed lull followed to quiet her emotions. She continued to lie still, knowing that Dr. Bell was at this moment trying to tell her husband what he refused to accept: There was no medicine, no surgery, no therapy, and no cure for their firstborn.

And Kent did not accept it. Now that the examination was completed and Dr. Bell informed him
that he could expect such recurrences at more frequent intervals, Kent could not keep the anger from
his voice.

"You must get him into a hospital," he said. "Au-
gusta, New York, London—anywhere in the world.
I have the money, Dr. Bell. I can get any amount
of money."

"Money has nothing to do with it," Dr. Bell said
firmly. "If I could help your child, I'd do so without
a round cent. There are some things beyond the
minds and hands of men. Only God's miracle can
grant life to your child, beyond infancy."

"Then you expect him to die soon?"

"Within the year," he answered, his voice barely
audible. "I said, except for a miracle. It's in God's
hands."

"Then Buddy Boy will die," Kent said, his words
cold with despair. "In this crazy overpopulated world,
what's one more baby to Him?"

"Everything," he answered. "He specifically mentioned the 'least of these.' He included all children,
particularly the sick children."

Kent's voice held contempt and vexation, "If you
can do nothing for him, I'll go where some doctor
can. I intend to take him to Dr. Mathews in Charlestown."

Dr. Bell nodded silently. He knew Dr. A. J. Mathews and he knew countless other reputable pedi-
atricians and heart specialists. He knew that Kent

143

would subject the dying infant to examination after examination in any suggested clinic. It was surely the father's prerogative, but was he so blinded by paternal love that he could not see the ultimate result? Dr. Bell loved the tiny boy himself and it pained him that Kent still believed money could purchase anything he desired, even life itself.

"I want you to understand, Kent," Dr. Bell said finally. "If anything under God's heaven could be done, I'd recommend it."

"All right, Dr. Bell, I accept what you say—that you can do nothing. But I'm not giving up. I'll try a thousand doctors if I think it will help."

"If you need me, call me," Dr. Bell offered. "I'll do what I can." He waited a moment and when Kent did not reply, he left him standing there, gazing into the crib.

        o   o   o

When the baby was five months old they took him to Dr. Mathews at the Children's Pediatric Center in Charlestown. They went with fear in their hearts and with almost certain knowledge what the answer would be. After only a few minutes' consultation with Dr. Mathews, following his examination of the baby, they knew his verdict. Nothing could be done.

"He has a congenital heart deficiency," the doctor told Kent, careful to avoid Jo's eyes, grave with this irrevocable burden. "Love him. Enjoy him. Thank God for him. I'm here if you need me, but I'm afraid nothing anybody can do will help."

"What could be done?" Kent asked, staking new

144

hope in the physician's remark. "What could be tried? Money is no question. A thousand, ten thousand, a million dollars—just tell me what can be done."

Dr. Mathews turned away briefly, his lips twitching ever so slightly. "I knew you would try anything anybody suggested," he said. "There will be suggestions; there always are. There may be doctors who'll advise you regarding methods of treatment or clinics you haven't tried. I'm almost positive, short of a miracle, that nothing can be done. This is beyond the hand of man."

"Then we'll start believing in miracles," Jo said.

"If nothing is done and if nothing does help him, how long do you give him to live?" Kent asked.

"I can't say," Dr. Mathews answered. "I'd rather not try to fix a time. We're not infallible."

"Nevertheless, Dr. Mathews, I intend to take him from coast to coast," Kent said stubbornly. "I'll never give him up."

Dr. Mathews offered his hand, first to Jo, then to Kent. "I wish you Godspeed in whatever you do. I'm sorry I can't help you. He's a fine little fellow."

They smiled at that, momentarily relieved, but when they went out into the corridor they held each other, crying their grief. Everything in the world had turned black. There was no hope anywhere.

They took him home that same day, but before plans could be scheduled for the next consultation the child died, exactly one month after Dr. Mathews' examination. Six months, ten days, and three hours old. Kent marked it in the baby book in the nursery, but Jo recorded it in the white Bible. Beneath the

entry marked DEATHS she wrote the date and his
full name, adding: Buddy Boy was in his seventh
month when he left us, but he is in the hearts of
his Daddy Kent and his Mother Jo forever.

o   o   o

Lizbeth had begun to despair of winning Jo to
Christ. But she went to the Wilson home the morning
following that of Buddy Boy's funeral. Though she
had hoped to read the Bible with Jo as they sat
in the nursery, Jo forbade her to open the white
Bible.

"It's not for me," she said. "I can't believe in
your God. How can you see His love in the twisted
bodies and tortured minds of babies?"

"Reverend Redmond mentioned that in his book
I brought to you," Lizbeth said. "Did you read it?"

"I read it and I burned it," she answered.

Lizbeth sat quietly a few moments and then spoke
gently, "Even so, I want to invite you to the tent
revival. It's been going on a week now. Reverend
Redmond asked about you last night and he wants
to see you. He'd come here if you'd invite him."

"I don't want to see Reverend Redmond, or any
other preacher," Jo said. "None of them can bring
my baby back to me and nothing else matters now."

"If I can help you in any way, call me," Lizbeth
said. "We'll keep remembering you and we love you.
Jo, God loves you and needs you."

Jo smiled then. "Why does He need me?"

"Because, Jo, you have so many natural gifts—a
gift of joy and laughter, a gift of understanding and
loving, and a gift for giving yourself. He gave you

146

these gifts. He needs them for His kingdom work."

But as Lizbeth left this house of unrest, she became embroiled in another tragedy. As soon as she arrived at the station, Walter Webb met her with the latest Loganville news—a crude statement that was making the rounds from mansion to hovel: Vi Shedd had gone crazy.

19

☐ WHEN CHARLEY SHEDD developed his idea of chaining Vi to his body, ankle to ankle, while they slept, he had not taken into consideration that Vi's mind might just as easily snap in daylight. The love he felt at first sight for Viola Murdock when she was sixteen, and he barely two years older, had not faltered in their thirty-one years of marriage. The sorrows they shared, having outlived their three children, had drawn them closer. Yet the grief had worn into Vi's emotions until the time came, a year ago, that Charley could not sleep until he literally locked her to his body. He believed she would break down at some indefinite time, but he had hoped to be present, a shield and a rock to this woman he loved.

And today, without warning, it had happened. About midmorning as she started feeding the chickens in the backyard, the first passenger train shrilled down the valley. At once she reverted to the day Cecil left, going toward the Wilson home in the Shedds' automobile. In a sudden moment of distortion she visualized Cecil at the crossing, his car stalled, and she ran toward the railroad, babbling, "Son, wait! Train coming, wait—"

When the train whistled short, short, then long, her foot reached the rail. But firm hands swiftly pulled her back to safety.

The hands belonged to Brother Presley who walked toward the Holy unto God Church. He had been walking slowly, meditating on his sermon prepared for that evening, when she rushed past him. Quickly grasping the situation, he ran to her and snatched her from the rail, with only seconds to spare. Afterward, he knew that his act had been entirely rational. He had moved, knowing he could reach the rail before the train passed.

The following day, at the recommendation of Dr. Bell, Vi was admitted to the state asylum. She went willingly, and knowingly, expressing hope for an early recovery.

"I can't imagine Charley batching," she told Dr. Bell, who came to the Shedd house to help send her away.

"While you're away I intend to see that he learns how to keep house perfectly," he promised. "Then when you come home he can take care of you royally."

She started to answer. As her lips formed a reply,

unexpectedly she screamed and two white-coated attendants quietly placed her inside the waiting ambulance.

Late that day Charley went to the Lambert house, still unable to believe the day's events. That her life had been spared filled him with unmitigated happiness. Anxious to appear properly grateful he praised Brother Presley for saving Vi's life.

"There's no way to thank anybody for such an act," he said, graciously accepting the cup of fresh-brewed coffee Lizbeth poured for him. "I guess I ought to apologize to him for what I've said about the tent meetings. I feel ashamed of it after what he did for Vi."

"I think an apology would be appropriate," Lizbeth urged. "I talked with Brother Presley just today. I found out just what I suspected."

"What was that?"

"Well, I know sometimes people do give their lives, knowing they'll die themselves, so that they can save another person," she said. "But I suspected in this case it wasn't necessary. Brother Presley saw the train in time to snatch Vi back from the rails. At least, he told me that. He said he knew if he could only reach the rail, he could rescue her and that's the way it happened."

"But he did save her," Charley said defensively.

"Yes, but he only risked his life," she answered. "See the difference, Mr. Shedd? Jesus Christ gave His life for me and for you and for everybody else. He didn't calculate that if He went only a little way up Calvary, only to the rail, lost sinners would

150

meet Him halfway and be saved. He had to cross the rail, to the very center, and actually die to accomplish salvation for all mankind."

Charley reverted to the old ground of spirited argument. "If Jesus lived and if He died like they say—well, I can't believe there wasn't some sort of calculation there, too."

"There was," she agreed. "He took the calculated risk. He died for the sins of all people, knowing many would accept His rare gift—the gift of eternal life. Not all are wise enough to understand that. In the Bible we're told a servant of God should be as wise as a serpent."

"If God turns me from heaven even yet, I can't forgive Kent Wilson. I never sleep a whole night for thinking of what happened. Before God would claim me I'd have to go to that hypocrite and tell him I understand all about how he needed another plaything. Cecil was a good Christian boy till he started following Kent."

"I felt the same way about Kent for a long time," Lizbeth confessed. "I tried to serve God with my heart full of hatred but such service bears no kingdom fruit. I had to forgive Kent. That was the good and wise thing to do."

"Then you think it's wise, running over to the Wilson house," he snorted. "Everybody in Loganville wants a house like the Wilsons'. Every woman wants to be like Jo. Looks like the whole world has gone crazy. So I'm expected to go to Kent and tell him it was all right for him to change my boy into a stranger in my own house."

"You remember, I talked with Cecil just before he died," Lizbeth spoke gravely. "I have every reason to believe he died in God's grace."

"You've said that a hundred times," he said. "But you never said why."

"Then I'll tell you now. Cecil made me promise to win you to the Lord so that the family could be together again someday."

Charley stood motionless, only his labored breathing showing his deep emotion. And then the decision was made.

"I'll have to see Kent," he said and he departed quickly.

           °   °   °

Two hours later Charley stopped at the Lambert house and called Lizbeth from her customary Friday evening ironing to relate his visit with Kent an hour earlier. As soon as she reached the veranda, she knew that everything was not as she anticipated. "Won't you come into the living room?" she invited. "Mother's resting in the kitchen. We could talk privately. You came about Kent."

"I just dropped by," he said. "I'll not come in; not got much to say. I talked to Kent. We talked a long time. I guess I went too far. I told him I'd buried the past, but I guess I went too far."

"I'm glad you witnessed to him," she said, puzzled.

"I reckon after you get to be a Christian, God won't let you rest with things as they are," Charley said. He waited a while, watching her face reflect her pleasure at this wonderful news. "I've got things fixed up with God. Now I feel responsible for Kent.

I feel like he's my third son. I guess I made a mistake there."

"A mistake? But how could it be wrong?" she asked.

"Because I made Kent mad at me before I left," he said worriedly. "I asked him to stop playing big rich hypocrite and turn back to God and live a sensible life."

Lizbeth did not reply for a while. She was stunned into silence, not only by his unexpected overture but because she knew that Charley had been sincere. It was the only way he could seek to win the lost for God.

Simon Peter could be nobody but Simon Peter. He spoke forthrightly and frequently he offended, because of the crude intensity of his devotion, and sometimes because of his doubts. Yet Peter was a Rock.

As Charley turned to go, lifting his hat in an unspoken good-night, she thought, Another Rock has been raised to His glory. Who knows what may happen now?

20

☐ THE AUGUST REVIVAL at the big tent was in its third week, with no sign of closing. It promised to run on into the fall months, as the tent revivals frequently did in Loganville. The husks on Charley Shedd's corn had turned from brilliant green to faded brown, toughening for the harvest. Soon all life would be gone from the plants.

Shriveling like my heart, Lizbeth thought, as she walked home from the bus station late Friday afternoon.

She had barely reached the mailbox when Reverend Redmond drove into the yard. He came often now, fitting easily into the household. Though his words and actions indicated a marriage proposal, Lizbeth could not accept this.

"My dear, you look tired," he greeted her gently, looking deeply into her eyes. He knew that she was troubled with indecision and that her tiredness sprang primarily from her unhappiness.

"I'll talk with your mother now. Go along, rest a while, then get dressed for church. You've plenty of time."

"I know I should be elated over Mr. Shedd's conversion," she said. "It's the most glorious thing that has happened to us since Cecil died. But somehow I feel as though the world had stopped. I can't explain it. I sound completely ungrateful."

He shook his head slowly. "It's the letdown that follows triumph. The mother of a new baby feels the same. It's the high pitch of ecstasy, the realization of one's hopes and dreams, funneling again to a normal level. What you feel after Mr. Shedd's surrender to God is perfectly understandable."

"You're full of understanding, Neal. And you are wondrously patient."

"Relax, Lizbeth, dear. Don't worry about me. I love you and I'll wait forever for you."

"Forever is too long," she said. "You need a wife to help you. I'm sorry I can't be that one. It wouldn't be right to marry you without love."

"I said I'd wait," he said firmly. "Now do as I say, or you'll not be able to go to the revival to-night."

They went into the house, Lizbeth going directly to her room. Before she rested or made any preparations for the evening, she knelt in prayer, asking God to help Reverend Redmond put her out of his

155

heart. Needless to expect a change of heart in her.

She prayed for Jo, a brief intercessory prayer, and she mentioned Kent. Here, too, a miracle would be required, for surely he was now more rebellious than Jo herself. He knew—or had known—God in His true omnipotence and Jo was apparently wholly ignorant in spiritual matters.

After a very brief rest and a quick shower, Lizbeth joined the others in the kitchen. Neal had prepared sandwiches, at the direction of Mrs. Lambert, who followed him about in her chair. Together they had spread a rather festive table.

"I'd never imagined any one man could have so many talents as Neal," Mrs. Lambert said, using his first name at his request. "Any time I look at him I realize what I've missed, not having a son of my own."

Neal glanced at Lizbeth and she managed a faint smile. Mrs. Lambert made no effort to conceal her matchmaking efforts.

"Feel better?" he asked Lizbeth.

"Much better, thank you," she said. "I believe Jo will find God somehow. But I don't know how. This past hour I just feel so."

"We can't anticipate God's power nor how He will work His miracles," Neal said. "Kent promised he'd come tonight."

"Why, Neal, what a surprise! And Jo? Is she coming?"

"She didn't say," he answered. "I wanted her to come with Kent, but she didn't commit herself. Incidentally, did she read the book I sent for her?"

Lizbeth paused momentarily. She had avoided mention of the book, not wishing to offend him, but she could no longer keep the secret. "She read it— and burned it."

"I wish Jo could have been with me the night I was called to Johnston after the tent meeting. Remember?" He looked from Lizbeth to Mrs. Lambert. "This businessman, a sales representative for a clothing company in Chicago, suddenly found death was near and he was without God." He paused thoughtfully, visualizing the scene in that shabby hotel room.

Oddly he remembered now that a bulb had burned out in the lamp on the old dark dressing table and the only lighting came from an overhead low-unit bulb in the bathroom. He remembered, too, the pornographic magazine lying on the worn red rug. He could still feel the impact of the murky green walls and the faded green draperies. The weariness of the room reflected the despair in the man's heart.

"He appeared obsessed with the Bible," Neal said. "He wanted to hold it while I read to him passages of God's promises. He seemed impatient of Jesus' promise of mansions. 'I've had mansions,' he said. 'I want the promise of God. I want Him there. I can't cross that river alone.' "

"How sad!" Mrs. Lambert murmured, her eyes showing tears. "Makes me wonder about his mother. Did she teach him? Or did he reject her teaching?"

"He didn't have time to tell much," Neal answered. "He kept repeating: 'Why didn't I read it? Why didn't I?' And then he asked, like a child, 'Will I be able to read the Bible in heaven?' "

"What did you tell him?" Lizbeth asked.

"I told him he could not only read it but he would meet the Author and the stenographers and publishers who worked with God on the Book. Even so, he held the Bible to his heart and died with it there. His last request was that the Bible be buried with him. The doctor arrived then, but he had gone into eternity, literally holding the promises of God."

"What a touching story!" Lizbeth mused.

He did not reply until after table grace and then he referred again to the book, *Are You Shutting God Out?* As though he had never considered it before, he spoke eagerly, "That's exactly the point. We're all afraid of death—deathly afraid of death. We've shut God out. I'd never realized it quite so much as at this moment."

A silence fell over the group. The clock on the mantel ticked on; the fat gray-striped cat, Moriah, nuzzling at Mrs. Lambert's thin slippered feet, purred softly. The coffee perking on the stove and the spiced apple pudding simmering in the oven filled the house with a cozy warmth.

"I think that text would be perfect for a sermon tonight," Lizbeth said, remembering that Kent planned to attend. She wanted also to divert attention from the moment, chiseled to the finest point for a romantic interlude.

"Thank you," Neal said, as he accompanied her to the veranda where he added, "I'd planned this evening to ask you to marry me, but I see very well your heart is not ready, not at this moment, at any rate."

"Neal, please understand, my heart will never be right again. Except for serving God."

He looked at her compassionately, not now as Neal, but as the Reverend Redmond. "Lizbeth, we can't divide our hearts into compartments. If you can't marry me, that's one thing, and my regret. But try to keep your heart warm to all human relationships. Follow God's will and He can employ your services more readily."

"I'll try," she promised.

He left then, with only a brief good-bye. She watched him stride down the stone path, past the evergreen rows, aromatic after a fresh shower before dusk. She saw him turn at the mailbox and drive away. She knew his good-bye contained a certain finality. He knew now as well as she that he could not marry a woman with a divided heart.

o o o

As Kent promised, he came to the tent that night. He sat at the rear right, a section where a light bulb flickered and went out during the choir's opening song. He had a full view of the pulpit, but the Reverend Redmond, if he searched ever so diligently, would be unable to identify him in the half-light. This pleased Kent. He had come, having made excuses to Jo, who would have laughed at him if she had known his true intentions. So here he was, welcoming the privacy, as well as the nostalgic atmosphere, of an old-fashioned revival meeting.

Now he knew that the unease he had felt since his marriage was traceable to a yearning for the old altars. Henceforth he vowed to keep in touch, to go alone sometimes to renew his vows to God. Jo might be one of those who could live her life without spiritual guidance, but a hunger, unsatisfied, incomplete, ate continually at his heartstrings. Now that he had recognized the difficulty, he would deal with it privately, not bothering Jo, and thus keep his promise of nonintervention in her rejection of God.

He listened intently while the Reverend Redmond delivered his sermon based on the text: "Choose you this day whom ye will serve; whether the gods which your fathers served that were on the other side of the flood, or the gods of the Amorites, in whose land ye dwell: but as for me and my house, we will serve the Lord."

Fathers were upbraided for their lax position in contemporary society, letting children rule the family. Mothers were rebuked for possessive, unwise love for their children. Lashing husbands for turning over their homes to their wives, consenting to a puppet position, he also upbraided wives for not supporting the head of the household.

And then came the call to repentance and salvation, to the turning from darkness to light. The sawdust aisle to the altar led many persons to God that night. But Kent left, slipping through a curtain, winding his way over the sanded grounds until he reached the path leading to the parking lot.

Going directly home, he determined to end the promise to Jo. Better to follow through his decision totally.

He drove several yards past Minnie Duncan's house

before he decided to stop here for prayer. He backed the car, got out, and knelt in her garden, now devoid of flowers, and taken over by weeds. Yet the beauty of the garden struck him as nothing had done in his life before. Unaccustomed to praying, he spoke to God conversationally. "God, I love Jo as I love no one else. But I can't go on without You. I'm homesick for the church. Guide me. Help me to help Jo. Amen."

He arose then and returned to his car, heavy with the remembrance that he had promised Jo, until death, that he would not impose his religious beliefs upon her. But now he realized it had been a promise consenting to her everlasting destruction. If he broke his promise, she would surely leave him. But neither could he bear to lose her forever.

21

□ LIZBETH WAS FIRST to hear of the estrangement in the Wilson household. Jo came to her early the next day, through a heavy rain, seeking a private talk with her, and Lizbeth left the station. They crossed the bus lot, jumping over water puddles to get into Jo's station wagon.

"We could drive as we talked," Jo suggested uncertainly, conscious of the Greymount bus ready to pull out, heading south. "Or if you're afraid of driving, we can just sit here."

Lizbeth smiled at that. She had never known a driver of greater dexterity than Jo, but the sallowness of her usually flawless complexion startled her. Her nervousness, her lowered voice, a mixture of despair and grief, baffled her and impatient to know why she

162

had come, she said, "Jo, you're a splendid driver, but let's just sit here and rest a while. Then you can tell me what bothers you. You talk. I'll rest while I listen."

"No rest in what I have to tell," Jo warned. "Kent and I have separated." She read the surprise in Lizbeth's face, then added, "He broke our marriage contract. His promises! We've separated." A sob broke into her brief accounting. "We had agreed that his religion would never dominate my life."

"Let's go a little slow," Lizbeth begged. "You've knocked me for a whirl. I know how Kent feels about you and I thought you felt the same about him."

"You talk of love," she said. "Love blossoms; it grows, but it can die. Lots of things kill love. Kent is so changed. He's going back completely on a promise he vowed to keep till death parted us. We both knew that was really all that could come between us—I mean our different beliefs. Of course, we didn't always agree about our baby. He wanted him perfect and I knew it was an impossible dream. I thought we should accept him as he was."

"I agree with you on that," Lizbeth said. "You should thank God for your child, just as he was given to you. Only God can grant life, and however warped a life may be, God can bless that life for a true purpose if only people trust His wisdom."

"Maybe so, but I can't believe in your God. It's all a myth. But I'm talking now about the promise—"

"Excuse me for interrupting, but tell me about the promise."

163

Jo fidgeted with the crocheted buttons on her mulberry rose suit. "He promised he would never interfere with what I thought about God," she answered. "He said he'd marry me as I was and his God didn't necessarily have to be my God." She looked at Lizbeth challengingly, the pupils of her eyes pinpoints of fire.

"Suddenly then he broke this promise," Lizbeth mused, remembering that he had attended the tent meeting. Who was she to counsel this lost, heartbroken woman when she had vowed, after Neal's parting last night, to avoid any meeting where he might be present in the future? She had done so for his sake, but where did God fit into her scheme? "Would you tell me why he suddenly decided this?"

"The tent revival," she replied, her voice sharp with contempt. "He came home in such a—such a fuss. He explained that he refused to let Joshua be a smarter man than he was." Jo paused, clasping and unclasping her delicate jeweled hands, and asked, "Who is Joshua?"

"A great Hebrew leader of the Old Testament," Lizbeth explained. "He was one of the twelve spies sent to scout the promised land."

"Oh. I thought he was a fertilizer dealer or a farmer. You know, Kent's obsessed with being the top man on Loganville's totem pole."

"Maybe the sermon last night will change that."

"It changed him all right," she said. "Lizbeth, I'd like you to go over there after I leave and pack my personal things and send them to me. I'll send you my address after I'm settled. I plan to return to North Carolina. Perhaps find a job with my former employer."

"You're leaving today?"

"Sunday afternoon—tomorrow," she answered, the weariness breaking her voice. "Tonight I'm staying at the Town Inn. I want twenty-four more hours—to think."

"I'll do this for you, if you must go, but I'll have to tell you this," Lizbeth said. "Christianity is revolutionary. Kent couldn't return to his altars and the altars of his good parents unless he did appear at war with himself, and with all opposed to what he believed. He wanted you in his camp, that's why he waged war—or so it seemed to you—to get you into his camp. Winning a soul to God is war, you know, Jo."

Jo's confusion, indecision, and heartache tore at Lizbeth's heart. "I want none of it," Jo replied. "Just tell me whether it's asking too much for you to send my things."

"I'll be glad to do this for you," Lizbeth promised. "You go on to the Inn and make yourself as comfortable as possible. It's rather primitive, the Inn—Wait a minute." She ran back to the station, the rain beating about her bare head, slicking down the lustrous honey-colored hair. She was back within minutes, cradling in her arms the small radio she had kept at the station since the first day she started work there.

"Now don't go over there and get too lonesome at the hotel," she said, pushing the radio into Jo's lap. "Keep something going all the time. You need

165

the company of people, you know."

"Thank you, Lizbeth. Thank you truly for just being you. You've been a bright spot in my life here in this town. Sorry I can't agree with you on everything."

Lizbeth smiled valiantly, despairing yet hoping for Jo in her need. "God be with you—even yet," she said, in reply to Jo's farewell.

22

☐ DURING THE BUSY SATURDAY noon hour, when four buses stopped in transit, Lizbeth remembered a salient fact which Jo should know. Strange that Lizbeth should have forgotten to tell her when she had come by the station two hours ago, that Neal had personally invited Kent to attend the tent meeting that night. If Jo knew, it might somehow help her understand her emotional dilemma. She hurried to the telephone booth near the front door.

Searching through the tattered directory she located the Town Inn number. Finally Jo answered in a voice pitched with caution and weariness.

"What have you done to yourself?" Lizbeth asked. "You don't sound like Jo."

"I've done absolutely nothing. I'm just lying here

in bed, listening to your radio. I'm glad you called, Lizbeth, I wish I could sleep. I've taken one sedative after another but I'm wide awake."

Chill fear for Jo chased through Lizbeth's thoughts. Jo, whose mother had tried to sleep away her troubles.

"I've something to tell you," Lizbeth said. "I thought you'd like to know. I forgot it while we were together. Kent promised Reverend Redmond he'd come to the tent tonight."

"Really, Lizbeth, I don't care. He can go, of course, but he'll not influence me." And Lizbeth heard the heartache and hurt in Jo's stricken voice.

"We all need God, Jo."

"Well, maybe your evangelist will preach again on demarcation," Jo said. "That sermon really made Kent fidgety. If his family were what people say, they surely produced a prodigal son."

"I'm sure the tent will be full of prodigal sons— and daughters," Lizbeth said. "The best Christian needs to attend revivals. I wish you'd come."

"Who, me? Never. Repeat—never!"

"Then I wish you'd listen to the sermon on WAGV," she persisted. "It starts at eight o'clock tonight."

"I might do that." Jo was reluctant. "I might, just to see what they say. They've changed Kent so much he doesn't seem like my husband. He's like somebody new."

"God's love does that if you allow Him to come into your heart."

"Maybe, but I'm listening out of curiosity," she reminded Lizbeth. "Kent has puzzled me from the

168

first, but now he's completely out of my depth."

"I'll call you tonight after the meeting to see if you're all right," Lizbeth promised.

"Thank you, Lizbeth. You never surprise me. I know what you'll say. You're entirely predictable and I love you for it."

Lizbeth returned to the station, thinking that Jo would be priceless to God's kingdom, if only she would surrender her heart to Him. And she knew that for this reason God had commanded her to bring Jo to Him. Yet she had failed. Turning her back to her customers she restacked the soup cans on the shelf, so that her emotional confusion could not be seen. She had failed in her promise to God.

Walking home at sundown she found a letter in her box from Vi Shedd. She welcomed the news that Vi had at last answered one of the many letters Lizbeth had written to her. She was glad to know that Vi was getting better every day. But her match-making efforts, heretofore conveyed by Charley, continued in this letter.

"I hope by the time I get home you're married and keeping house," Vi wrote. "I have some good recipes I'll give you when I'm home. They're in my cookbook. I started pasting favorite recipes in a scrapbook after I was married."

She did not mention Cecil. Nor did Mr. Shedd talk of Cecil now. Their silence seemed a token of faith in God. And that itself was one of God's miracles wrought in two weary hearts. But not Lizbeth's. There had been no miracle, no change.

"Mrs. Shedd hopes to be home by Christmas."

She brightened with effort as she handed the letter to Martha Lambert. "We'll have a homecoming party for her here at our house. How would you like that?"

"I think it's fine," she answered, then hesitantly, "And, Lizbeth, could we invite Neal? It would be something he'd enjoy with all his heart. You know how he feels about you and our friends."

"Yes, we'll invite him," Lizbeth promised. "Mother, I'm leaving for the tent a little early. I'm sure Mrs. Webb will be here any minute."

"Go ahead," she urged. "Tell Neal to hurry back to see me." Lizbeth could not confess to her mother that she needed God in this hour, that her heart was in turmoil. She knew nothing to do except to stop at Minnie Duncan's prayer garden for a moment's respite.

o   o   o

A dampness from the early dew that evening had settled the dust, and the foliage in the prayer garden smelled faintly of fresh-cut lawn grass. Tough weeds and briers had taken over the once beautiful flower beds. Though Minnie's flowers had dried up a year past, it yet impressed one that a life built on faith in God was imperishable.

Strange that Lizbeth had not stopped to pray here until now. Kneeling she spoke simply: "Father in heaven, first I ask salvation for Jo and for those other lost people I know, and those I do not know. But I come also for myself. My heart is withered, like these summer flowers. Renew my heart. Grant me a freshened heart as the waters that purify the

Ocmaha River. Then I shall be able to serve Thee unreservedly. Amen."

She rose then and hurried toward the tent, finding a vacant seat four pews from the front, on the left side. She had hoped to arrive unrecognized but Charley Shedd, in his place in the choir loft, nodded toward her. She silently asked about Vi and he nodded his head smiling. She's better, his eyes told her.

Mr. Shedd is a Christian, she was thinking. Mrs. Shedd is well on the way to recovery. Kent, the local prodigal son, has returned to God and the altars of his fathers. Yet—yet there is still Jo. And there is—Lizbeth Lambert—unsettled of mind and heart, unhappy, not yet pleased with God's answers to her prayers.

As the organ sounded the first notes of "I Am Thine, O Lord," a song she had always loved, she prayed again: "Father, let me not grow into a bitter complaining woman, whatever my future may be."

23

□ KENT SPENT THAT SATURDAY afternoon critically surveying his estate instead of returning to the house where unrest fermented so noticeably. As he started home at sundown, his mind was more settled and satisfied. He would remain here—he and Jo would remain here—and he would increase his holdings year after year. He would remain here— no longer neutral about faith and worship and God's kingdom. Nor could he remain careless of Jo's nonfaith.

His mind stilled by this decision, he ruminated the second thing he had planned to do. An hour after he left the store at three o'clock, he had staked the spot where a warehouse, a longtime dream, would be built. Having made the decision, the blueprint took shape and form as he visualized the long brick structure, the width and length of a city block, with neon-lighted windows facing the town. With a population increase, Loganville was ready for progress, and if he coaxed the movement toward the Wilson farm, Kent knew that the value of his estate would soar.

But as he entered the familiar kitchen, he sensed at once that the house was empty. Even before he found Jo's note under the sugar bowl, beside the coffee urn, fear seeped through his entire being. Then he seized the scrap of paper and read it fearfully. Angered for a moment, he tore it into bits. But quiet realization banished the anger and he knew that now he faced a decision he could no longer evade. A born decision-maker, a wizard at handling business and financial problems, he now groped for a solution.

Jo had gone. A momentary whim, a sudden, hasty impulse? Not Jo—not that willful girl he had married.

Nobody else knew because that was the way she wanted it, as though the shared secret would alleviate the pain. "We'll not let the people know— for a while," she had written in her note to him. "Other people always make so much of such things. We know why this had to be. There is only one reason, but they'll invent so many different versions it will hardly seem like us at all."

Now the finality settled heavily upon him. He paced the length of the house, feeling its emptiness, the utter desolation. At last he recognized the extent of his loss. He had lost everything.

Going to his car, he drove away from the house,

not looking back, no longer caring to inspect his possessions. It was nothing to him now.

He turned from Loganville Road, drove a mile past the Wilson Grain and Feed House, turned without reason onto Banks Street, and drove five miles, to the road forks at Coal Mountain.

Then acting again without reason, not caring what he did, his speedometer clicked off sixty miles an hour until he reached Little Points railroad crossing. With no train in sight, he raced across the intersection and arrived at First Church when the bells started ringing.

He stopped at the back of the church and went to his son's grave. Not once had they visited the grave together and since his death, they had avoided using the pet names, Buddy Boy or Little Cole. He became known to them as "our baby" or "our child" or simply "he" and when they spoke of his burial place in the wind-swept cemetery at the rear of the church, they referred to it as "the grave." He stood a while by the miniature mound, his head bared, staring at the low stone bearing an opened Bible on the pages of which was written: SUFFER THE LITTLE CHILDREN TO COME UNTO ME.

Standing beside the small grave, Kent appeared the facsimile of every handsome, successful businessman who daily graced a thousand advertising pages throughout the nation.

I have nothing but myself to give to God, he mused. I have lost everything precious to me, but now I return to God. I have lost everything here, but I have gained heaven.

He gazed toward the Wilson estate, and the lighted campground arrested his attention. They are assembling now, he thought, watching headlights flicker in and out among the pine foliage. That was where the transformation started, the restoring of his soul to himself and to God. He loved Jo, he loved her yet, but not even she could separate him from the love of God.

I'll go over there now; I'll return and thank Reverend Redmond, he thought, keenly realizing how much he had floundered in lostness on earth and perhaps in eternity as well.

He drove back over the railroad crossing and at Grape Avenue, as he started to stop at Mrs. Duncan's garden to pray, he saw someone kneeling there. Though her back was turned, he finally recognized Lizbeth Lambert. He drove on wondering what lost soul she prayed for now. Had she lost patience with Jo?

24

☐ THE INSCRUTABLE WAYS of God were never more evident than Saturday night in Loganville. Reverend Neal Redmond had spent seven days preparing a soul-searching sermon for the final evening's service. All day the billboard held the announcement: HEAR YE! THE SALVATION PLAN.

He appeared in the pulpit, his Bible opened to Romans 1, his text marked: "I am not ashamed of the gospel of Christ." Though he planned to read the first chapter of Romans, he turned instead to the Fifty-first Psalm. This should be his sermon and he had no definite reason for knowing why, except that God had ever so gently spoken, "This, my servant— this tonight." Accordingly he read the entire psalm, and repeated at the end his chosen text: "Create in me a clean heart, O God; and renew a right spirit within me."

The choir followed with an old song, sung with all the technique that hours of rehearsal could effect. Charley Shedd, the most loyal of all who served at the tent, sang with a grateful heart and a full rich baritone.

Today he had visited Vi and learned that the doctor permitted her to listen to the broadcast every night over the little radio Charley carried to the hospital soon after her admission. For a while the radio had been stored in the locker room, but now that she had improved, Vi listened an hour each night. This was her hour and he sang as though she sat in the congregation, his deep voice singing the familiar words:

> I've wandered far away from God,
> Now I'm coming home;
>
> o   o   o
>
> My soul is sick, my heart is sore,
> Now I'm coming home. . . .

Quickly he searched the congregation for a face, present last night, and present again if his prayers had been answered. He was rewarded with a view of Kent, sitting in the middle row, near the front. At the same time he glanced at Lizbeth and he frowned. Lizbeth was crying; crying quietly—but crying. She had not cried since Cecil had died and he wondered what had happened. His voice faltered on the second stanza. There was so much trouble. If God took away one sorrow, man in his own undoing gave root to another.

After the song ended, the Reverend Redmond stood silent, his eyes looking straight before him, over the crowded tent where many stood in the aisles and at the rear. He saw Lizbeth and he wondered why she wept. He looked at her briefly, sensing a sharp pang of agony for her. And then he spoke, his voice deep and clear.

"David pleaded for a new heart," he said. "David desired a new heart in order that he might attain the grace of God, and that he might stand tall in the presence of man. God gave David a rare kind of manhood so that he has been distinguished through the ages as a man after God's heart." He paused thoughtfully, sensing the gravity of what he would say next.

"Yet David sinned. My friends, David committed a terrible sin." He was aware that most of the congregation had heard the story of David's defection, of Bathsheba's lasting sorrow, and of David's agony when their child died. They knew that part well; that part they considered a sensation, akin to thousands of modern incidents. But some did not know the full meaning of David's final consolation, wrought by his faith in God.

Nor did these people know that in the faith of David and in the faith of his own fathers, Neal Redmond had found the will to live when death seemed desirable. "Like David's son, my own children cannot return to me, but I can prepare to go to them. Their mother is there now. After they died in that flaming apartment she grieved until God in

His mercy called her on home, only one year later. Our home, at one time so happy, was torn apart in less than one hour. That, my friends, is an example of the thin line that separates you and those you love from disaster.

"Assuredly, God is the healer; He is the soothing adhesive that makes life livable and sometimes joyous. But there is a price to holding on to the Almighty God. If one is to know the full joy of the Lord, he must pray daily: 'Create in me a clean heart, O God; and renew a right spirit within me.' Let Thy will be my will."

At this point Jo switched off the radio and snatching her purse, she raced toward the campground. But for Lizbeth's telephone call, informing her that Kent would be at the tent tonight, she would not have turned it to the revival broadcast. She had merely wanted to hear what Kent would hear, and that prompted by angry curiosity. But the sermon had been prepared for her surely, surely. Now she saw everything clearly; now she understood.

Breathless, excited, she remembered a shortcut which led through the back alley, going by Grace and Riley Stevens' house, and passing beneath the covered bridge. She hoped to reach the church unseen, for as yet none but Lizbeth and Kent knew that she was leaving him, not to return.

The night train screamed as it rocked around the mountainside and headed toward the Little Points railroad crossing. It was the same train that had crushed Cecil's speeding car into a mass of twisted steel.

Give me time to get there, she cried silently. Time, time. . . .

She arrived as the Reverend Redmond closed his sermon and came to the altar to offer the invitation. With a cry of thanksgiving she slipped down the aisle, over the sawdust floor, and clasped his hands in hers.

"I've come," she murmured. "God's will must be my will. I understand now. Now I can prepare to go someday to be with our Buddy Boy."

"You've made a wonderful decision," he said consolingly as she knelt at the altar, and to the congregation, "My friends, we should all be big enough to say, 'God's will must be my will.' " He met Kent part way down the aisle, coming to the altar, and he led him to his wife's side. And then he beckoned others to the altar of God.

After the last "Amen," Lizbeth Lambert made her way down the aisle. Since she had left Mrs. Duncan's prayer garden she could not control her weeping, but in her heart God had wrought a miracle. In her grief for Cecil, she had seen as through a glass darkly but now she knew that he was safe with God. Her work was here, unfinished, and God had led her to the Reverend Redmond. She saw the way now and she knew it was right—if she could take the first step.

She glanced at Charley Shedd, sitting in the choir loft, and he nodded his head. He knows how I feel tonight about Neal, she thought. He and Vi and Sally and Jo, bless them all, they knew he loved her and now she knew she loved him! Finally, her heart pounding, she hurried down the sawdust trail and slipped her hand into that of Reverend Redmond.

"I've come, too," she whispered. Now she could offer her heart, renewed and refreshed like the waters of the Ocmaha. "If the invitation is still open to your heart, my Reverend Redmond."

He clasped both her hands in his. "The invitation to my heart is always open to you," he whispered. "I told you I'd wait. I'd have waited an eternity for you."

Smiling happily now, her face radiant, she glanced at Kent and Jo, standing arm-in-arm, smiling at each other and at the countless friends who came to wish them well. "They're happy now," Lizbeth said.

"Very," Neal answered. "The mystery and the power of God's redemptive love is beyond all understanding."

DATE DUE

MAR 1 2 1968			
DEC 5 1968			
JUN 1 8 1969			
NOV 5 1979			
MAY 1 5 1980			
NOV 2 2 1981			
GAYLORD			PRINTED IN U.S.A.